RAVES FOR The Better to Kiss You With

"4 ½ stars… It was so well written that I never once doubted it. The last part of the book was very exciting and full of threat and suspense."
—*Inked Rainbow Reads Reviews*

"4 ½ stars… I really enjoyed the writing style of Ms. Osgood and hope to read more by her in the future. Her voice was so clear and the emotions she brings forth are so rich. I kind of don't want this book to end."
—*Molly Lolly Book Reviews*

"*The Better to Kiss You With* is a heady paranormal romance with a Canadian Gothic atmosphere. Cherry blossoms bloom in a moody, misty spring while terrible notes turn up and computers can haunt more than any presence."
—*Friend of Dorothy Wilde Book Blog*

RAVES FOR Huntsmen

"*Huntsmen* is a delicious mix of urban fantasy and queer feminist romance."
—*Autostraddle*

"Blazing hot."
—*Just Love Reviews*

"… gosh did I love every intense second of it."
—*G. Jacks Writes Blog*

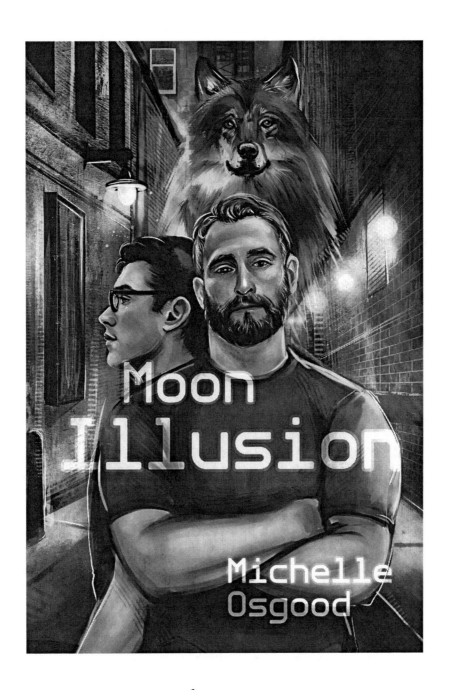

Moon Illusion

Michelle Osgood

interlude press • new york

Copyright © 2018 Michelle Osgood
All Rights Reserved
ISBN 13: 978-1-945053-56-6 (trade)
ISBN 13: 978-1-945053-57-3 (ebook)
Published by Interlude Press
www.interludepress.com

BOOK AND COVER DESIGN by CB Messer
COVER ART by Monika Gross
10 9 8 7 6 5 4 3 2 1

interlude ♣ press • new york

To Trever.

Nothing vast enters the lives of mortals without ruin.

—*from* Antigonick *by Sophokles,*
trans. by Anne Carson

Some readers may find some of the scenes in this book difficult to read. We have compiled a list of content warnings, which you can access at www.interludepress.com/content-warnings

Chapter One |

NATHAN POPPED AN APPETIZER INTO his mouth and moaned theatrically as the balsamic-covered cherry tomato burst on his tongue.

"They spare no expense on the booze at these things," he commented around his mouthful to his co-worker Cris. The Musqueam woman lifted her champagne glass in a grateful salute. "But there's never enough to eat," Nathan continued. "You'd think, if anything, you'd want to serve *more* food so people don't get as drunk."

"Unless, my dear, the whole idea is to get people drunk," an amused voice countered from behind him. "That way," she continued as she lowered her voice to a whisper, "they won't think so hard about their wallets when they bid."

Nathan swallowed hastily. "Dorothy," he said with a grin as he turned to face their hostess. Well into her seventies, Dorothy wore a bright red gown, with diamonds that dangled from her ears and more that dipped into her décolletage. "You are radiant!"

"You clean up nicely yourself, young man." Dorothy kissed the air on each side of Nathan's cheeks. "Now don't be rude." She rapped him smartly on the forearm with her fan—a concession to the July heat or an accessory, Nathan wasn't sure—and turned to face Cris. "Introduce me to this divine creature."

Nathan cleared his throat. "Dorothy Ho, meet Cristina Sparrow—Cris—a new hire in our department. Mrs. Ho," he informed Cris, "is hosting tonight's fundraiser for the university library."

"A pleasure to meet you." Dorothy held out her hand.

Cris clasped it in both of hers and beamed. "You have a beautiful home, Mrs. Ho. Thank you for putting this together for the library! Nathan said you've done so for the last few years."

"Oh, it's nothing." Dorothy waved her fan. "Any excuse to get this handsome man in a tie." She batted her lashes at Nathan, who rolled his eyes. "Though if you don't mind, I need to steal him away for a moment."

"Not at all." Cris glanced around the lavish second-floor study they'd found themselves in. "I need to find the bathroom anyway."

"Down the hall and to your left," Dorothy directed.

Cris lifted a hand in thanks and slipped through the other guests in the direction Dorothy had indicated.

"Nathan."

"Yes, ma'am." Nathan straightened and held out his arm. Dorothy slipped hers into his and nudged him in the direction of the mansion's large wraparound balcony.

Outside, the air was thick and hot. Nathan was glad he'd passed over a suit jacket for a fitted vest, though, as a slow line of sweat made its way down his back, he wondered if the vest was a better choice than the more loosely fitted coat. Then again, the light gray vest and matching pants combined with the soft lilac of his dress shirt, and the darker purple of his tie brought some color to his pale skin and highlighted the blue of his eyes. And, there was actual product in his hair—Ryn's doing, of course.

"I heard you brought a date with you tonight," Dorothy said, as they reached the glass rail.

Nathan made a noncommittal noise.

"A fine gentlemen, or so I've been told," Dorothy continued. "I can't say I've had the pleasure of meeting him myself."

Nathan huffed out a breath. "It's not like I've been hiding him."

"No?"

"No." He squared his shoulders. Really, the only problem with Dorothy and Cole meeting was that they'd like each other too much. And between the two of them, they'd know too much about him. "I'll introduce you."

"I know you *date*," Dorothy said as they went down the stairs, referring to Nathan's intense dislike for monogamy. "And maybe I don't understand that, but I don't judge it. However, in all the time I've known you, you've never avoided introducing me to one of them."

"I'm not avoiding." They eased through the crowded first floor toward the nearest set of flung-open patio doors. Nathan had left Cole by the pool and suspected his boyfriend wouldn't have gone far. "Does it look like I'm avoiding?" He only half paid attention to Dorothy's answer; he was seeking one guest among those gathered around the pool.

There. Standing by the large poolside gazebo that hosted the restaurant-grade barbeque, Nathan caught the steady lines of Cole's profile three quarters turned away: the strong, bearded jaw and the broad shoulders.

Across the pool, as though he felt Nathan's approach, Cole stilled, turned. The noise of the party, of the laughing, half-drunk guests, faded into the background. Cole's gaze spanned the crowd and the water and found Nathan's eyes.

This far away Nathan couldn't see the details, but he knew Cole's honey-gold eyes softened. He knew the corners of his mouth ticked up—just a little on the right. He could see the way Cole's stance opened. *Unfurled*, offered a dumbstruck part of himself, foolishly in love.

He realized he was staring across the pool at Cole with a moronic grin plastered on his face and hearts in his eyes. Ears hot, Nathan cleared his throat and escorted Dorothy around the pool.

As though sensing the significance of the woman on Nathan's arm and perhaps *literally* sensing that significance—as a werewolf, Cole's senses were far beyond what Nathan could comprehend—Cole broke away from the trio he was conversing with and moved easily through the crowd to meet them. The wine red of his tie was the only splash of color against his black suit jacket and his crisp white shirt.

"Mrs. Ho." Cole took Dorothy's proffered hand. "Nathan speaks very highly of you."

"He's told me next to nothing about you," Dorothy replied.

Cole caught Nathan's gaze over Dorothy's head, and Nathan rolled his eyes. He hadn't said *nothing*.

"Then I look forward to telling you myself," said Cole.

"No time like the present, is there?" Dorothy hooked her arm around Cole's. "Nathan, be a dear and fetch me another drink?"

"Yes, ma'am." Nathan sketched a bow and headed for the bar. Maybe he'd find another plate of appetizers. Maybe Dorothy and Cole wouldn't speak about anything but the weather.

Chapter Two |

"...SO SHE'S TALKING TO ME about our numbers for the second quarter, but all I can think is what it'll take to get her number, you know? Ass like that." Male laughter rang out as the speaker cupped his hands in front of him. His wedding band glinted in the light. "Not sure what she expected, showing up to the meeting in that skirt."

"Presumably to be treated with professional respect from her coworkers," Cole interjected mildly. He lifted his beer and took a sip as the laughter faltered to a few awkward chuckles.

The speaker, a large, goateed man, blustered. "Look, buddy, it's just a bit of fun. She wouldn't give me her number anyway."

"I'm not your buddy." Cole set down his glass and did nothing to hide the disgust he felt. "And I don't see the fun in sexual harassment."

The group of men shared stunned, guilty silence. Cole didn't wait to hear another excuse. He tucked his hands into his pockets and left, angling away from the party.

He needed a minute to himself to breathe in the sweet summer air and to breathe out the anger that simmered in his stomach. A whiff of menthol told him that he wasn't the only one sneaking away for a break, and he followed the scent.

Kiara had made her way to the tennis courts—this house had not one, but two—and was smoking a slim, menthol cigarette in the dark.

"Some party," she said, blowing smoke from her maroon lips.

"Some party," Cole agreed. Nathan had roped the entire pack into coming, insisting that the more bodies at the party, the better it was for the library.

C'mon, just pretend you're super wealthy and want to bid on art, he'd cajoled. *There's free booze!*

Cole tilted his head back. They were far enough from the lights of the house and the party lights strung through the surrounding trees that the stars and sliver of moon were crystal clear in the night sky. He shut out the sounds of the party and focused on the quieter noises of the grounds: the wind rustling through the leaves, the secret darting of rodents through the manicured lawn, a low whicker from the other side of a thick hedge. Cole startled in surprise and turned to his sister. "There are horses next door!" The warm, musty scent was so unexpected that he hadn't identified it earlier.

"Yup." Kiara shook her head. "Imagine living in this city and having so much space you can keep more than one horse."

"Imagine having more than one tennis court."

"Imagine having a pool."

"Imagine that it comes with a hot tub."

"Imagine trying to keep Dee from living in your hot tub." They broke into good-natured laughter. They were both exceedingly fond of Nathan's best friend, their cousin Jamie's partner, Deanna.

"Ah, well." Kiara took one last draw on her cigarette, and butted it out, and tucked it into a napkin to dispose of later. "I'd say *one day* but I doubt this is what either of us are working toward."

"I wouldn't say no to a hot tub." He couldn't think of a better way to end a shift—a work shift or a wolf shift—than sinking into deep, frothing water.

Kiara snorted. "We can't fit one in the apartment."

"You're spending a number of nights with Ryn," Cole pointed out. "We could convert your room."

"Over my dead body."

They spent a moment in companionable silence before Kiara gave a hefty sigh. "All right, better head back before Nathan hunts us down."

Arm in arm, they walked up the hill. Kiara broke off to find a garbage can and another drink, and Cole went to find his date.

He spotted Ryn holding court on the balcony. The werewolf was surrounded by a crowd of admirers and flashed Cole a cheeky grin. Ryn's long hair hung loose, inky black against the white dress shirt, and as glossy as her oxfords.

Cole lifted his hand in a wave and followed the bright floral trail of Dee's perfume into the first floor of the gigantic house. It was a safe bet that if he found Dee, he'd find Nathan as well.

Sure enough, he found them both downstairs. Nathan was bending over a pool table with his butt in the air and his lips screwed tight as he lined up his shot. Dee stood to the side with her own cue loose in one hand and her other arm around Jamie's waist.

Nathan sucked in his breath and took his shot. The white ball leapt forward and missed every other ball on the table before rolling smoothly into the far-right pocket. Nathan swore, and Deanna cackled mercilessly.

"You're so bad," she crowed.

"You're no better," Nathan retorted. He stood back from the table and gestured at the scattered balls. "You haven't sunk a single one either."

"Not yet." Deanna smirked and sauntered forward. "I've got it this time, though." She glanced at Jamie behind her. "My good luck charm's here."

"No helping!" Nathan yelped, as Dee fished out the ball. He glared at Jamie. "No sneaky," he lowered his voice, "werewolf moves."

The butch werewolf turned wounded eyes—the same golden brown color as Cole's, as Kiara's—onto Nathan. "It hurts me that you think I'd cheat."

Nathan sniffed and moved to stand beside Jamie as they watched Dee take her turn. Jamie slung her arm around his shoulder and pulled him close to her blue-suited side.

His chin propped in his hand and an unconscious smile on his lips, Cole sank down to sit on the stairs.

He'd loved Nathan since the first moment he saw him, bare chested and bloody, blue eyes wide and wild with a mixture of fear and fury as he attempted to face off a deadly werewolf with nothing but a flare and a stick. It had been hopelessly stupid, and gloriously brave, and Cole's heart had tumbled right off the cliff.

He'd expected the feeling to fade; the rush of adrenaline that came with the shift to wolf and back again was surely responsible for the intensity of his attraction to the lanky librarian. It hadn't. If anything, his feelings had deepened the more he came to know Nathan. Smart, sharp, and adamantly independent, Nathan was all Cole ever wanted.

For all Nathan's bravado and flirtation, however, he was quite skittish. Cole knew if he came on too strong he'd send Nathan running for the hills. So he'd kept his feelings to himself, had let Nathan grow comfortable with their friendship. And if all that was between them had been friendship and shared love of their friends and Cole's packmates, Cole figured he'd have been content. But one weekend trapped in Nathan's apartment with danger lurking outside and Cole in Nathan's bed had blurred the lines. A kiss had crossed them.

Dee, perhaps reaching a delicate balance of booze and confidence, took her shot and sunk not one, but two striped balls. She let out a whoop and leapt into Jamie's arms for a smacking kiss.

Nathan made a noise of disgust and looked up to see Cole on the stairs. He grinned and gestured for Cole to join them. "C'mon," he called. "I need *my* good luck charm!"

"No sneaky moves!" Dee wriggled free of Jamie's arms and pointed a warning finger at Cole.

"Wouldn't dream of it." Nathan stuck out his tongue.

Chapter Three

"I DIDN'T REALIZE LIBRARIANS WERE this loud." Cole's voice was low in Nathan's ear; his arm was warm around Nathan's waist. They stood at the back of the crowd on the patio, where, now much later in the night, most of the party-goers were gathered.

"Hey," Nathan objected. "Most of these people aren't librarians."

"No?" Cole's hand spread against Nathan's back.

"No. Most of them are donors. Besides." His breath caught when Cole's hand trailed around his hip. "Librarians are quiet."

Cole backed Nathan into an unlit corner flanked by lush foliage.

"How quiet?"

"Uhh…" Nathan had trouble forming a sentence as Cole's beard scraped across his jaw. Cole's hand slid across Nathan's thigh, and Nathan bit back a groan. "I'm at a work party," he managed finally—a weak protest, and one they both knew he didn't mean as his hips hitched against Cole's.

"I guess you'll have to be very quiet…"

Nathan's head fell back against the wall of the house. His eyes closed behind his glasses as Cole pulled open his belt, then the button on his slacks. "I'm only allowing this," he said with whatever semblance of dignity he had left as Cole's teeth sank firmly into his neck, "because

I know your stupid werewolf hearing will tell you if anyone comes around that corner."

Cole growled, a sound wholly inhuman, and Nathan shivered. His hands dug into Cole's muscular shoulders as Cole's hand slipped into Nathan's briefs and gripped his cock. Nathan swallowed hard as Cole's hand began to move and let the thrumming of the music match the hot thrum of his blood.

It didn't take long. Cole knew exactly how to twist where so that Nathan arched, careless of his shoulders that dug into the stucco and stifling his cry with his fist.

As the shock of pleasure rolled into easy bliss, Nathan sagged with a punch-drunk smile. "You make a pretty good party date," he told Cole.

"I do all right." Cole grinned, already having pulled a handful of napkins from his pocket to wipe them both clean.

"How long have you been planning this?" Nathan asked, amused, as he tucked himself back into his pants.

"A while," Cole admitted, brown eyes twinkling.

"Party's bound to wrap up soon. Why don't we go home, and I'll return the favor?" Nathan leaned forward and caught Cole's lips with his. Cole hummed and pressed Nathan back, fitting his thigh between Nathan's legs so Nathan could feel the hard length of him.

"Please." Cole nipped at Nathan's jaw.

"You smell like semen," Kiara accused, her eyes narrowed, as she waited by the door.

"What? No!" Nathan squawked, cheeks flushing bright red.

"You do," Jamie confirmed, her nose wrinkling.

Cole held his hand out for Dee, who was wheezing with laughter while she balanced on one foot, as she tried to get her foot back into the nude heels she'd worn with her midnight-blue party dress.

Nathan glared at them—sparing Ryn, who'd winked appreciatively— and turned as their host entered the foyer.

"Thanks again, Dorothy." Nathan hugged her. "Seems like this year's Silent Summer Auction was another success."

Dorothy squeezed him tight. "Take care."

"I will." Nathan stepped back to allow Cole to bend, though not as much as Nathan had, to hug Dorothy.

"It was nice to meet you." Cole straightened.

"You as well." Dorothy beamed. "You all come by any time."

Nathan had a sudden flash of Cole snaking his hands down Nathan's pants against the side of Dorothy's house, and a guilty flush rose to his cheeks.

"We'll do that," Cole promised. Nathan was probably imagining the hint of smugness in his voice.

"THAT WAS FUN." COLE TOOK Nathan's hand on the way to Nathan's car. Kiara had driven the other three friends, and Nathan waved as they piled into her car.

Nathan smiled. "I'm glad you had a good time."

Cole unlocked the door, and Nathan slid into the passenger seat.

"It is awfully convenient that my werewolf boyfriend is sober enough to drive us home," Nathan commented, as Cole settled into the driver's side. "Last year I had to wait forever for a cab, and that was even using the rich-people-bump-the-line priority number Dorothy gave me."

"Happy to help," Cole said easily and started the car.

"You are, aren't you?"

Cole looked quizzically over at Nathan. "Yes?"

Nathan shrugged, a little self-conscious. He was usually better at controlling his brain-to-mouth filter, even after a few drinks. With Cole, Nathan had trouble keeping his guard up. Being around Cole made him question why he had a guard up in the first place.

"You just—you *are* happy to help." Nathan tried to elaborate while Cole put the car in reverse and eased them out of the tight parking space. "I don't know if I've ever met anyone as happy to help, if they can, as you. It's good." All nonchalant-like, he kept his gaze off Cole and focused on the towering trees that lined the driveway.

Cole laughed, low and warm. "Thank you." He reached over, squeezed Nathan's leg, and kept his hand there as the car merged onto Marine Drive.

"And you even accept complements gracefully," Nathan sighed, dropping his head against Cole's shoulder as his hand found Cole's on his thigh and wrapped their fingers together.

"Sorry I'm so perfect."

"No, you aren't."

"No." Cole grinned. "I'm not."

Buzzed enough to ignore the twinge in his neck as he watched the lights speed by, Nathan let his head lie against Cole's shoulder. It was hard to believe that just over a year ago he hadn't known werewolves were real and now he was dating one—seriously, not even, seriously he was dating a *werewolf*, but he was dating a werewolf *seriously*.

It was weird, but good weird, Nathan acknowledged, curling his fingers tighter around Cole's. A lot of things in Nathan's life fit under the "good weird" category. None of the rest of the things were as bizarre as werewolves, but if anyone could embrace an entirely non-normative lifestyle, Nathan figured it was probably him.

"Are you going to stay over tonight?" he asked Cole as they turned toward Nathan's Mount Pleasant neighborhood.

Cole shook his head. "Night shift tomorrow." When he switched from days to nights, he tried to stay up all night until late morning so he wouldn't be as tired for his shift. That meant not staying at Nathan's while Nathan tried to sleep.

Nathan pushed back against his initial flash of disappointment and nodded against Coe's shoulder. He in no way begrudged Cole's schedule as a paramedic. In fact, the odd hours Cole worked probably did more to help Nathan ease into the idea of being in the kind of relationship they were in—a serious one—than anything else the eternally patient Cole had done. With Cole's schedule sometimes the opposite of Nathan's, Nathan could enjoy his time alone without feeling as though he was neglecting Cole.

However, Nathan slept better when Cole stayed the night. He didn't jerk up from nightmares, clammy with cold sweat, with his heart pounding in his chest. He usually slept straight through to his alarm in the morning and woke up rested.

It's all right though, he comforted himself. Tomorrow was a Saturday. If he didn't sleep, he could nap later. He had less trouble with naps.

"I'll come in with you, though," Cole said.

"Yeah?" Nathan wriggled as close as his seat belt would allow and nipped at Cole's ear. "You'll have a nightcap?"

"Sure." Cole let out a slow breath when Nathan sucked the lobe of his ear into his mouth. "We can call it that."

"Excellent."

Chapter Four |

NATHAN'S HANDS WERE FIRM AGAINST the bare skin of Cole's hips, holding him in place against the large island that dominated Nathan's kitchen. Cole's fingers gripped the wooden countertop, and he gave a full-body shudder as Nathan bent and swallowed the length of Cole's cock.

On the counter behind Cole, their drink glasses sat neglected; ice slowly melted into gin. Nathan pulled back to swirl his tongue around the head of Cole's cock. Cole's hips made an abortive jerk forward. A groan fell from his lips as Nathan pulled off fully to lick his way up Cole's shaft.

"How—" Cole broke off; the muscles in his thighs twitched when Nathan took him in again. "How are your knees?" he gasped.

Nathan looked up. Cole's cock was heavy on his tongue. *Really*, he conveyed with his expression.

"I know," Cole began, as Nathan began to move in earnest with his gaze still rolled up to Cole's. "But you're kneeling on concrete and I don't want you to—" Nathan cupped and stroked Cole's balls as he drew Cole farther into his mouth.

Nathan made a soft noise of approval around Cole's cock and returned his attention to the task at hand—or mouth. *Mouth* and *hand*, he thought, with a mental smirk, and pressed his fingers against the skin behind Cole's balls. Cole tensed above him; the muscles in his thighs trembled. Nathan sucked harder, flattened his tongue along the underside of Cole's crown, and used his other hand to jerk Cole's shaft in time with the movement of his mouth; the glide over Cole's hard flesh was slick and easy.

Cole's chest heaved; a ruddy flush bloomed under the forest of dark curls. His head fell back, his hands splayed wide, and the first pulse of come flooded Nathan's mouth. Nathan swallowed eagerly and pulled back, continuing to jerk Cole off as come landed in hot streaks across his face until Cole went lax against the island.

Nathan ran his hands down Cole's thighs, smoothed the coarse hair, and settled back on his heels. More than a little pleased with himself, he licked the corners of his lips, where come slid toward his mouth, and gave Cole a second to recover.

Once he regained his breath, Cole stroked Nathan's hair and tilted Nathan's head up to display the mess of his face. Nathan's lips were parted, wet, and swollen red. In the kitchen light, Cole's come was pearly and gleaming against Nathan's cheeks and forehead. Though Cole was completely naked, Nathan had discarded only his vest. He still wore his dress shirt and slacks and had barely taken the time to loosen his tie.

"Thank you," Cole murmured; his honey-gold eyes roved over Nathan's face. He rubbed his fingers against the shell of Nathan's ear, then slid them through a line of come on Nathan's cheek. Nathan smiled; a glow of warmth settled over him at the soft reverence in Cole's caress.

Cole bent and kissed Nathan, slowly and deeply, before he straightened and stepped around Nathan toward the bathroom. "Stay there," he said. He returned with a damp washcloth for Nathan's face. Nathan reached to take it, but Cole shook his head, and lifted Nathan's chin so he could clean Nathan himself.

Nathan closed his eyes and let the soft cloth move over him, enjoying the residual heat from the hot water. When Cole finished, he dropped the cloth to the counter and helped Nathan to his feet.

Nathan winced as he rose. Cole hadn't been wrong; the concrete was hell on his knees. He would have grabbed a cushion off the couch, or at least a folded towel from the bathroom, but when they'd got in the door all Nathan could think was how badly he wanted to taste Cole against his tongue, and all else had fallen to the wayside.

"Are you all right?" Cole asked, as he handed Nathan his glasses.

Nathan rubbed his knees. "I'll be fine in a sec." The ache would vanish in a minute or so, and it had absolutely been worth it. He pressed his lips to Cole's and hummed in pleasure when Cole wrapped his arms around him.

"Are you sure you don't want to stay?" Nathan asked. Cole's arms around him felt so good. Nathan thought he could slide into sleep right there—if Cole was cool holding him up all night. Cole probably could, though it wasn't an ideal scenario. Nathan's bed upstairs, on the other hand…

Cole shook his head.

"I know." Nathan stepped back and picked up one of the tumblers. He took a quick drink of gin and let its sharpness carry away the last lingering taste of come. "It's fine, really," he assured Cole, catching the worried line of Cole's mouth.

"If you're having trouble sleeping again—" Cole started.

"I'm good." Nathan set down the gin, cupped Cole's face in his hands, and soothed with lips and tongue until Cole softened beneath him. "I just like having you in my bed."

"Next time," Cole promised. He circled Nathan's wrists with his hands.

"Sounds good." Nathan glanced at the clock on the microwave and eased back with a smile. "I'll let you get dressed then, I guess."

"Thank you. I appreciate it."

"Any time." Nathan winked. He dropped onto one of the bar stools that flanked the island as Cole began to gather his scattered clothing. How Cole's tie wound up on top of the fridge he wasn't sure, but it probably wouldn't be the last time.

"Any plans for tomorrow?" Cole asked, as he buttoned his dress pants.

Nathan spun his tumbler between his fingers. "Thinking about joining Dee and Arthur at the dog beach in Kits. Ryn might come, too." Deanna, his best friend, and her dog Arthur were two of Nathan's favorite people, or person and dog. Ryn, a werewolf who was dating Cole's sister Kiara, was rapidly joining those ranks.

"That sounds fun." Cole's voice held a trace of wistfulness.

"We'll make sure you can come next time," Nathan promised. Cole loved his job, but the hours could be terrible for his social life.

"Deal." Fully clothed, Cole cut a devastatingly handsome figure with his suit jacket and tie slung over one arm.

Nathan set his glass on the island and rose to give Cole a final kiss—with a suggestive hint of tongue. Cole groaned in protest and squeezed Nathan's ass in rebuke as he stepped back. Being a werewolf, Cole's refractory period was essentially zilch, and Nathan knew—from a handful of memorable and exhausting nights—that Cole could, quite literally, fuck for hours. Nathan tried not to take advantage of that fact *too* much.

"Now go to bed." Cole fixed Nathan in his gaze. "You won't have any fun tomorrow if you can't keep your eyes open."

"Yeah, yeah." Nathan waved him off. "Go save lives."

Cole pressed one last kiss to Nathan's forehead and let himself out of the apartment. Nathan locked the door behind Cole and, after a moment of indecision, pushed the swing lock in place as well. He'd installed it a few months ago, after the chaos of February and the Huntsmen, and still wondered if it was an overreaction.

Then again, having Kiara and Ryn attacked in his building's parkade by a suddenly not-so-mythical group of humans dedicated to hunting dangerous werewolves meant that his paranoia was probably justified.

"You're not crazy if they are actually out to get you," he reminded himself. Now that Cole was gone, the apartment seemed uncomfortably empty. The converted industrial loft, with floors and walls of thick cement and impossibly high ceilings, had been a haven of space and privacy after the hell of student housing in his late teens and early twenties. These days he looked at it with detached calculation.

Third floor. Narrow front hallway, bathroom off to the left. Kitchen just beyond. Opens into a living space, bank of windows at the end. The bedroom's a small loft up the stairs on the right, over the kitchen. Closets and cupboards are the only hiding spaces. One exit, the front door. Good soundproofing. Easy to defend. Hard to escape.

This observation was beyond ridiculous, considering that the closest Nathan had ever got to tactical military training was playing *Call of Duty*, except that as soon as he'd started seeing things that way, he couldn't stop.

He'd mentioned it to Dee once. She'd looked at him sideways and quirked a sad smile. "Welcome to the reality of living in an unsafe world."

Uncomfortable with her apparent nonchalance, Nathan had tried to shrug that off. "It's stupid. It's not like there's a psycho werewolf or a wacko human with a gun around every corner."

"No, but they're around some."

"How do you stand it?"

She'd smiled again, the same sad smile that didn't reach her green eyes. "The world isn't safe for women, for nonbinary folks. What's one more monster waiting in a dark alley?"

Or in the bar, or the bedroom you share, or your workplace, Nathan finished silently. As a cis white dude, he knew he walked through the world differently than Dee or Ryn. It was humbling to be reminded of that, and he hadn't brought up the issue of safety with Dee since. After all, if she could live all her twenty-seven years having to be hypervigilant about her safety, the least Nathan can do is shut his mouth when he'd only experienced fear once.

In the kitchen, Nathan finished the last swallow of his gin and, after a fuck-it shrug, he downed Cole's. The gin burned his throat, and he let his eyes slip closed as the heat of it expanded in his chest. If he had another, he'd sleep, probably. The gin combined with the free-flowing champagne at the party—and the lack of a real dinner—would be enough to knock him firmly on his ass.

A nervous jitter lingered in him, which the alcohol had been unable to still. "Besides," Nathan said aloud to the empty apartment, "I can't drink myself to sleep every night."

And that was true; he couldn't. He didn't, for the most part. He'd figured out an alternating pattern of sleep aids; he didn't want to get reliant on any one thing, nor did he want his need for them to be obvious. Everyone had enough going on without having to worry even more about Nathan.

So he'd alternate booze with weed with sleeping pills. He'd tried the more holistic approaches: exercise, herbal tea, hot baths. They hadn't worked though, and Nathan had gotten desperate. Self-medicating had worked. And it was fine, Nathan insisted to himself. He wasn't reliant on any one. He wasn't abusing his sleep aids—he was using them in moderation, smartly.

Nathan swung into the living room and crouched to open the small drawer on the coffee table where he kept his vape and pot paraphernalia. A joint was left behind from when Dee had been over last, and Kiara had surreptitiously added another lighter to their pile, as if they didn't know she occasionally snuck onto the roof to smoke menthols and brood.

Usually Nathan would grab his vape and head to bed, but tonight the walls of his apartment—*Third floor. Narrow front hallway, bathroom off to the left. Kitchen just beyond*—seemed to be closing in on him. The thick concrete seemed no longer protective, but suffocating. Nathan took the joint and a lighter and headed for the roof. He'd channel Kiara. Surely the Alpha Bitch Extraordinaire never got nightmares.

Outside, the summer heat remained unabated, and Nathan tugged irritably at the collar of his shirt. He'd left the tie downstairs, but he hadn't thought to ditch the shirt as well.

He lit the joint and took a long drag. The fingers of his free hand nimbly unfastened buttons until the shirt hung loose. The slight breeze against his bare skin was better than nothing, and Nathan tipped back his head and took another drag.

The smoke was harsh on his throat, and the harshness was somehow comforting—a reminder of his humanity, perhaps, of the fragility of his human body, of his human mind. Not that he needed the reminder.

Werewolves existed, and he couldn't talk about it. A young girl had nearly died under him with her skin ripped open and her blood pumping against his hands, and he hadn't been able to talk about it. He'd debated going to therapy. He wasn't an idiot. He had enough friends in social work to know how important therapy or counseling could be after a trauma. But he couldn't shake the fear that if he started talking about some of it, he'd talk about *all* of it.

Instead, he clammed up, adjusted. After all, he'd read *Twilight*, played *Wolf Among Us*, watched all the *Underworld* movies—it wasn't as though he couldn't imagine a world with the supernatural. He'd deal.

Nathan exhaled and watched the lazy twist of smoke rise with the light of Vancouver's downtown high-rises an out-of-focus glow in the background.

I should come up to the roof more. The high curled gently through his system. It was quiet up here, almost still. He'd sleep when he got downstairs; he was sure of it.

At a sudden clatter to his right, Nathan jerked back. The joint dropped from his hand.

Close, closer than anyone should have been able to get without Nathan noticing, a man rose from where he'd crouched and retrieved a pair of gleaming metal tools. Nathan's thoughts scattered. Fear was as sharp and metallic on his tongue as the tools were in the stranger's hands.

"Sorry about that," the man said sheepishly. He lifted the tools, and they were garden-harmless.

Early in the summer, several rows of a rooftop garden had appeared. Nathan hadn't seen anyone tend to the plants, but they'd flourished. This must be the mysterious gardener.

"It's fine." Nathan fought to slow his breathing. *Not a threat*, he told himself. *Not a threat*. He even recognized the Indian guy—a neighbor from the building.

"Still, didn't mean to startle you. Have a good night." He lifted his hand in a friendly wave, revealing a gold bangle on his wrist, and gently closed the door behind him.

Nathan's heartbeat took longer to slow than his breathing, and by the time his panic had faded entirely he'd lost track of the rest of the joint. Since he'd left his phone downstairs and hadn't had a flashlight on his keyring since he was twelve, he gave it up for lost.

"Some relaxing smoke," he muttered. He turned from the view and hoped the sudden rush of adrenaline hadn't burned through too much of his high.

Once he reached his floor, exhaustion hit like a freight train. It took all his energy to lug himself up the loft stairs and yank off his clothes before he fell face-first into bed. Nathan wriggled, moving so that his face wasn't pressed directly *into* the pillow, and was out like a light.

Chapter Five |

HE RAN THROUGH THE WOODS.

His breath burned in his lungs; his sneakered feet pounded against the ground. Branches whipped, caught on his shirt, nearly tore off his glasses. A howl, sudden and chilling, broke through the sound of his labored breathing. He ran faster, raced toward it, desperate to get there before—

The trees stopped. He stood at the edge of a clearing that was awash in the light of the full moon. Three bodies lay in the center—three forms unmoving. His pulse pumped, a living thing that throbbed in his ears to an unfamiliar beat. He took a step forward.

The black wolf stopped pacing. Across the clearing from Nathan, it stood calmly behind the bodies and watched him with eyes that glowed an uncanny orange.

Nathan's hands clenched into fists at his sides. He should have weapons: a large branch or an emergency flare lit and blazing. He had neither.

The wolf threw back its head and howled.

Nathan started forward. He had to get to them. He had to get there before someone else.

At a movement to his left, he jerked away, stumbled over his own feet. On his right, a hand steadied him; its grip was sure on his elbow.

"It's okay," Kiara said. Her honey-gold eyes matched Cole's. Diminutive, with a strength that belied her size, she kept her grip firm.

"We're here." Cole, it was Cole who'd appeared on his left. "It's okay," Cole echoed his sister; his deep voice seemed calm.

Relief left him weak. They were here. It would be okay.

Across the clearing, a door opened, and a woman stepped through. The door was familiar; its nondescript beige paint was an exact match for the door in Nathan's office at the university. He frowned; a line of trepidation snaked cold down his back.

"Mr. Roberts." The woman's voice carried easily across the clearing, clear as if she was standing only feet away. "If I could have a word." Her hair was long and dark. In the moonlight he couldn't see the color, but knew, with a horror that expanded slowly in the pit of his stomach, that it was the deep-red of dried blood.

"No." His protest caught in his throat. "No, no I don't want—"

She stepped to the side of the door, and two crouched men, dressed head to toe in black swept through. The guns in their hands glinted in the light of the moon

No.

Two shots, swift and silent, and Kiara and Cole dropped.

Nathan rocked back, off balance and unsteady. "No." It came out a moan, low and wounded.

"We need to take the lycans, but these two are yours."

Now he stood beside the three bodies in the center of the clearing with the Huntress at his side. More men in black spilled through the open door; they moved with the cohesion and practiced ease of a unit who'd cleaned up before. Two of them lifted Cole's limp body, and Nathan tore his gaze away.

Another pair came forward and gathered Ryn. Nathan watched their body be dragged away, refused to look down, knew in the sick pit of his stomach what he would find.

"These two are yours," the Huntress reminded him. She gripped Nathan's shoulder and spun him around so his eyes met her merciless ones. The bite of her nails sharp even through Nathan's T-shirt, she dug her fingers into his shoulder until he looked down: Dee with her blond curls strewn in disarray over the damp grass, her dress torn, her collarbone gleaming wet and red; Arthur beside her with his neck twisted at an impossible angle and his golden coat slowly darkening with Deanna's blood.

Nathan's knees crumpled, and he hit the ground hard enough to jar every bone in his body. Pain flared in his mouth; the bitten tip of his tongue was hot as he tasted blood.

The Huntress stepped away, followed her men back toward their door.

The wolf jogged past Nathan. Orange eyes fever bright, it cast one lingering glance over its shoulder at Deanna before it slipped through the door behind the Huntsmen.

Nathan ripped off his shirt and pressed it against Deanna's torn shoulder. Cold against his hands, blood soaked instantly through the fabric.

Cold. The blood was cold.

He reeled back, scrambling against the wet grass. He was too late. He was too late to help any of them.

"Dee?" Jamie's voice called out uncertainly from the surrounding woods. "Dee?"

Nathan curled into a ball; anguish was a thick rod that pierced him from his throat to his stomach. He couldn't speak, couldn't answer Jamie, as she called out again; her voice was moving farther away.

Deanna's upturned hand lay close to Nathan's face. Her nail polish was the color of a spring violet.

Nathan screamed.

A SECOND. IT TOOK A second that stretched into eternity while he fought against his bedsheets with the ferocity of a desperate man before Nathan realized where he was.

Bedroom. Second floor, loft apartment. No exit on this level.

He sucked in a huge breath, then another, before he let himself fall back against the bed. His legs were twisted in the navy sheets; his skin was pale and cold, sheened with a layer of sweat.

The blackout curtains on the apartment's large bank of windows let in little light from the street outside, but Nathan could make out the reassuring shape of the small potted succulent Cole had left on the bedside table one day. Nathan focused on the outline of the stubby leaves; their cheerful plumpness never failed to remind him of Deanna.

Deanna. Alive. Ryn and Cole and Kiara uncaptured. Jamie home safe with Arthur and Dee.

Nathan's breathing slowed. *Just a nightmare.* The panic in his chest began to dissipate, though a sick feeling of dread lingered. He sat up and pressed his fingers into his closed eyes, tried to force back the afterimages of the dream.

He should lie down again, try to sleep through the rest of the night. It worked, sometimes. Other times he slipped back into the nightmare—or into a new one. The thought of going through that again, of seeing his friends dead or taken, made anxiety creep up his throat.

He squinted at the display on his phone to check the time. Four twenty-three a.m. Not too bad. Almost four hours of sleep. The sun would be up soon. He slept better with the sun up, which was stupid, because it wasn't as if bad things didn't happen in the daylight, but some primal part of his brain assured him it was safer.

He'd get up now, fuck around on the Internet for a few hours, and nap in the afternoon when he got back from the beach.

Chapter Six |

"Did you sleep at all?" Deanna asked.

Nathan scowled behind his prescription sunglasses. He supposed he was grateful that Deanna had waited until after they'd left her apartment and her partner behind to pester him. Not that he didn't adore Jamie, because he did—especially when she'd made them eggs Benedict for brunch that morning and swapped out the ham for avocado on Nathan's—but some stuff was best friends only.

When Nathan didn't answer immediately, Deanna sighed. She slipped her hand into Nathan's as they headed toward the dog beach. Nathan squeezed her fingers and hefted her beach bag more securely over his shoulder.

When they left the sidewalk and hit the grass, Arthur quivered, straining against his red leash and matching collar. Deanna laughed and unclipped the leash. The second he was free, Arthur was off like a shot, across the grass and down the stairs to the beach. Nathan and Deanna followed at a more sedate pace.

"Ryn said she'll meet us down there." Deanna adjusted the wide brim of her straw hat. In a breezy sundress the color of daffodils, strappy white sandals, and large round sunglasses with matching white frames, she looked the picture of a lazy summer Saturday—in Hollywood.

Nathan looked much less put together in a pair of old shorts and a plain black T-shirt. Already he regretted the choice of color as the early afternoon sun beat down. He and Deanna had applied a generous amount of sunscreen before leaving her place, and Deanna had tucked the bottle in the bag Nathan carried so they could reapply it.

"Cool." Nathan jogged down the cement stairs. He held out his hand to Dee once he reached the bottom; the final step was a weirdly uneven height above the sand. As he helped her down, he scanned the beach. Ordinarily Arthur was easy to spot, racing across the sand by the water, but this time Nathan couldn't see him.

The beach was crowded, of course. Since this was one of the few dog-friendly beaches in Vancouver and Kitsilano was such a dog-friendly neighborhood, it looked as though everyone and their furred best friend had had the same idea as Deanna.

Nathan lifted a hand to shade his eyes as he and Dee walked down the sand. Ryn should have been easy to spot as well. An ex-lover from Kiara's past, Ryn had been thrust into their lives on a wet night in February, when the drag show they'd been performing at, with Jamie, Deanna, and Kiara in the crowd, had been infiltrated by the Huntsmen. Nathan had seen Ryn perform as Terence Stallion, and his shock at having his friends show up at his apartment in the middle of the night, accompanied by his favorite drag king who was—surprise!—also a werewolf, had been quickly quashed by the announcement that the werewolves were being hunted and they needed somewhere safe to hide.

Somewhere safe was Nathan's apartment, for *days*.

In that time, Nathan had had the chance to get to know Ryn: their pronouns she or they, a lone wolf with no pack to speak of, a genderqueer Korean-Canadian hair stylist with an attitude and stubbornness to match Kiara's. Nathan found a lot to like about Ryn. When it was revealed that the Huntsmen were after Ryn because of their lone-wolf status, Ryn had agreed to join Kiara's pack in a dramatic showdown with the Huntsmen that had taken place at Nathan's workplace.

So now the werewolf pack that was somehow a part of Nathan's life included Cole, Kiara, Jamie, Deanna, and Ryn. Nathan supposed Kiara would let him join, if he'd asked, but something held him back. It wasn't distrust, exactly, but maybe discomfort.

Before Nathan could analyze that thought further, Dee tugged on his arm. "Found him," she said and nodded toward the far end of the beach. Shaded and rockier, it was less crowded. Arthur stood at the edge of the water, barking happily at another dog behind him. As the second dog emerged from the shadows, Nathan gave a start. No domesticated dog, the wolf that loped easily toward the golden retriever had a pale gray coat, nearly white, and was easily three times the size of Arthur.

Ryn.

Beside him, Deanna gave a muffled squawk that managed to hold both laughter and dismay. "Oh, boy. If Kiara finds out, she's going to lose it."

Nathan couldn't disagree. Alpha of the pack, Kiara took her duties very seriously. Number one was keeping the existence of werewolves a secret. Unlike the other wolves, Ryn had grown up without a pack and without anyone to enforce the rules put in place by GNAAW—the General North American Assembly of Werewolves, the werewolves' governing body. And so Ryn operated according to their own set of werewolf rules, which drove their lover Kiara to dizzying heights of frustration.

"I won't tell if you won't," Nathan said as they headed into the shadowy side of the beach.

Ryn watched them approach and gave a quick wink before racing playfully after Arthur. No matter how often Nathan watched his friends go from human to wolf to back again, it was still weird as balls to see a wolf wink.

"Make sure you two stick to this side of the beach," Deanna called after Ryn. She took the bag from Nathan and spread out the blanket she'd packed. "The last thing we need is someone freaking out because our wolf scared their Pomeranian."

Nathan, meanwhile, had pulled out his phone and was Googling large dog breeds. "It's cool. We'll just say Ryn's a Kugsha."

"A what?" Deanna sat and arranged her skirt prettily over her knees.

"'A Kugsha, or Amerindian malamute, is a large working dog'," Nathan read. "'The thousand-year-old breed originated in America and is well-known for the dogs' intelligence and independence'."

Deanna snorted. "That sounds about right."

He settled onto the blanket beside her and leaned back on his elbows while they watched Ryn and Arthur play-fight and frolic in the ocean.

If he ignored the fact that one of the "dogs" had beaten his ass soundly at *Injustice* three nights ago, it was a normal beach day. Deciding there was no reason it couldn't be, Nathan grabbed one of Arthur's toys from Dee's bag and hauled himself up from the blanket.

Arthur heard him coming, gave an excited bark, and danced around Nathan's legs until Nathan wound back his arm and threw the toy as far as he could into the water. Arthur hurled himself after it.

Ryn made their way more leisurely to Nathan and, once they were close enough, planted their four feet in the sand and gave a furious shake. Nathan yelped and jumped back, but not before Ryn managed to spray him with the water that clung to their pelt.

"Seriously?" Nathan protested. Ryn parted their mouth, their tongue lolled in something close to a grin, and they pressed their side against Nathan. Nathan grimaced at the sensation of Ryn's still-wet fur against his bare legs, but gave them a quick rub while Ryn wound around him, like a giant cat.

The toy clutched in his jaws, Arthur barreled up to them. He dropped it at Nathan's feet and politely sat down, though his entire body trembled with anticipation. Ryn gave a soft bark of greeting to Deanna, who waved her hand in acknowledgement as she flipped through her copy of *bitch* magazine. Ryn made another doggy grin and echoed Arthur, sitting with every appearance of obedience at Nathan's feet when he picked up the toy.

"Are you gonna fetch? Who's a good doggy? Who's a good doggy?" Nathan cooed as he waggled the toy in the air. Arthur's tail pounded furiously against the sand, Ryn responded with the flattest look they could manage as a wolf. Now it was Nathan's turn to wink and before Ryn could tackle him to the sand—it looked as if they were giving the thought serious consideration—he lobbed the ball toward the ocean. "Go get it, pups!"

Ryn lunged after the toy, Arthur was hot on their heels, and the two of them splashed back into the water.

LATER, HIS ARM SORE FROM throwing, Nathan dozed with this head in Deanna's soft lap. She stroked his hair idly and watched their tireless companions race each other up and down the surf. Ryn's presence threw the other dogs into a frenzy, as they couldn't figure out if the strange wolf was pal or predator.

"Are you still looking for others?" Dee asked.

"Hmm?" Nathan blinked his eyes open behind his sunglasses.

"You know." Dee nodded at Ryn as they led a pack of a half-dozen dogs charging into the waves after a Frisbee. "Were-things, etcetera."

Wary of where the conversation was headed, Nathan gave a small nod.

"You find anything?"

He sighed. "No. Nothing concrete." But that didn't mean they weren't out there. If werewolves were real, then what else was hiding?

"Unicorns are kind of cliché," Dee said. "Centaurs though—that would be cool." She wiggled her eyebrows at Nathan. "I'd bang a centaur."

"Really?" He pulled his sunglasses down his nose.

Dee blushed. "I dunno! Maybe. If she—or he—was a particularly handsome centaur."

"Jesus." Nathan pushed his glasses back up. "If I find them, I'm not telling you."

"Hey!" Dee pushed him off her lap, and he rolled onto the blanket and folded his hands under his head.

"Fine. But I don't think Jamie would be into sharing you with a half-horse person."

Dee considered this. "She might make an exception. Maybe I'll add centaurs to my list."

"Please tell me you don't have an exception list. I thought that was something only straight people did."

"Not everyone wants to be as open as you," Dee chided him. "Monogamy is a perfectly acceptable relationship choice and style."

"A boring one."

"Oh, I'm not bored," she said with a coy smirk.

Nathan laughed. "Fine, you two are the exception."

"I thought you didn't like exceptions," Dee teased.

Nathan figured it best not to respond.

"But actually," Deanna said, seeming a little wistful. "I've always hoped the Ogopogo was real."

"The what?" Nathan rose up on his elbows. "Who's the Ogohobo?"

"Ogo*po*go. I forget sometimes that you're not from B.C."

"Thank you." Nathan pressed a hand to his chest. "I'm touched, honestly. Takes a lot to get the 'burta out of the boy."

"The Ogopogo is like, Canada's Loch Ness monster, but with a better name, and I've always felt like it'd be way more friendly. It's supposed to live in Lake Okanagan. When I was a kid, we'd spend summers in Penticton and we'd freak out every time we went swimming in the lake—'cause it *could* be seaweed your feet touched, or it could be the Ogopogo!" She smiled at the memory.

Nathan leaned toward her. "But would you fuck it?"

Dee took her bare foot and pushed him right off the blanket.

"I'VE GOT A CLIENT AT four, but does anyone want to grab some ice cream?" Now human and fully dressed in a pair of ripped gray jeans and a loose-fitting T-shirt with the arms cut off, Ryn dropped down on the blanket beside Deanna. With long, black hair that fell to mid-way down their back and dark-brown eyes under a pair of strong eyebrows, nothing about Ryn resembled the pale wolf.

Nathan shook his head. "No, thanks, I've got some stuff to do at home." Nap, he had to nap. Though it wasn't much past two, exhaustion was creeping up on him, and his eyes were grainy. At this time in his work day he usually picked up a double espresso from one of the many coffee shops on campus. His bruised and bloodshot eyes would make him no different than the thousands of other students pulling all-nighters. As it was, he was glad for the shield of his sunglasses.

"Mmm, ice cream." Deanna stretched luxuriously. "I think there's a two-scoop double chocolate raspberry chunk calling my name."

"That's very specific," commented Ryn.

"Dee knows what she likes." Nathan patted Dee's thigh. "Also she'll flirt with whoever is at the counter to try to get extra toppings," he informed Ryn. "So keep an eye on her."

Ryn raised their eyebrows. "They'll give you extra toppings if you flirt?"

"Sometimes." Deanna grinned.

"I bet I can get more free toppings than you." Ryn slid their gaze challengingly to Deanna.

Deanna eyed them speculatively. "Game on."

"Loser buys."

"Deal."

Ryn stood, then reached down to help Deanna to her feet.

Chapter Seven |

NATHAN LET HIMSELF BACK INTO his apartment with a weary sense of relief. Since the insomnia started, his apartment had become more of a haven. He didn't exactly feel safe there yet, but when he was at home, even if he wasn't sleeping, he was free of the constant scrutiny he'd come to expect from his friends and, lately, his coworkers as well. He'd been caught one too many times dozing off in his office or stumbling bleary eyed into the kitchen for caffeine.

Get it together, he reminded himself, not for the first and probably not for the last time that week. He would, he knew. He rolled with the punches. He was a rolling-with-the-punches kind of guy. So maybe the punches these days had, *ha ha*, supernatural force behind them, but that didn't mean he couldn't keep rolling.

It was just taking him a bit longer than it used to, that was all.

Nathan popped his head into the fridge and pulled out a container of leftover pad thai. He dumped it into a bowl and stuck a cover over its top before sliding it into the microwave. While it heated, he rinsed the container and tossed it onto his precariously piled box of recycling. The plastic container hovered on top of the pile. Nathan held his breath. It was going to stay...

It fell.

The microwave beeped, and Nathan groaned. He left the container where it was and grabbed the bowl of thai. Sitting on one of the stools at the kitchen island that served as his table, he shoveled the noodles into his mouth using the pretty floral chopsticks that had been a gift from Dee four Christmases ago. He'd take the stupid recycling out once he'd eaten. As Jamie so often reminded him—and the pack and probably anyone who'd listen—self-care wasn't just face masks and ordering in, but also taking care of basic household chores like the recycling.

Then he'd nap.

HE TOOK THE GARBAGE WITH him as well, and by the time he went to the garbage and recycling room he was yawning widely every other minute.

His phone buzzed in his pocket as he stepped out of the elevator onto the building's main floor. He was exhausted enough that he was tempted to ignore it, but the now ever-present worry—*what if it's an emergency?*—had him juggling the recycling box and the garbage bag into one hand so he could reach for his phone with the other.

It was a picture text from Dee. She flaunted her two-scoop double chocolate raspberry chunk, with what looked like added chocolate drizzle *and* flakes, while a good-natured Ryn stuck their tongue out in the background and held a single-scoop tiger stripe topped with gummy bears.

I WON! Dee captioned, unnecessarily.

When do you ever not? Nathan replied. An ellipsis bubbled up while Dee typed a response. Focused on the screen, Nathan continued forward on autopilot, absently pulled open the door to the garbage room, and walked through.

His left foot skidded out from under him, and he had a split second of realization, *I am going to fall*, before he did.

Chapter Eight |

NATHAN FLUNG OUT HIS ARMS to catch himself, but it wasn't enough. His palms slid against the floor; his forearms and butt landed with enough force to bruise before his head cracked against the cement floor. Stars burst across his vision. He had one breathless, suspended moment of relief that he was relatively intact until pain radiated like a halo from the back of his skull.

Nathan groaned. His eyes blinked open. *Ow.*

He sat up gingerly. His hands and arms were wet with something dark: a viscous liquid that was the unpleasant color of blood. *Ew.*

Now he'd have to shower before his nap. And, maybe, the way his head pounded sickeningly, he'd also have to throw up the pad thai he'd just eaten.

He'd let go of the garbage and the recycling as well as his phone on his way down. They all seemed to have landed clear of the mess that Nathan slipped on, but empty containers were strewn across the floor.

Careful of his sure-to-be-bruised body, Nathan eased himself up. When he wobbled to his feet, the smell caught him—hot copper, like a penny left sitting in the sun.

Not looks like *blood, but* is *blood.*

The pad thai threatened to come up then and there. Nathan gritted his teeth against the swell of nausea, closed his eyes, and breathed through his mouth. He realized his mistake instantly when the heavy scent coated his throat. He gagged and lurched to the side. He grabbed the nearest recycling bin to steady himself and took several deep breaths through his nose. CARDBOARD PAPER ONLY the bin announced. Nathan focused on the crisp shape of letters until the immediate need to puke passed. He wasn't ruling out puking later. In fact, he suspected it was likely.

After one more deep breath, Nathan steeled himself and turned.

Blood, more than he'd ever seen, more than he realized was *possible* to see, coated the floor like spilled paint. Five liters. Just over five liters—that's how much blood could be in the human body. His brain helpfully offered up an image of a plastic, four-liter milk jug and a second one-liter carton. When he thought about it like that, with the neat, sanitized whiteness of the two-percent milk he used to drink as a kid, the amount seemed terribly innocuous, hardly anything. But the amount on the floor, the amount that pooled on the concrete, that drew his eyes unerringly to its center, there was nothing innocuous about that, nor about the body.

It was a *body*. That was one thing Nathan was certain of, even if the rest of his reality was slowly tilting sideways. It was a body and not a person, because people couldn't survive losing all that blood—*four point seven to five point five liters, depending on size*—just as they couldn't survive losing their heads or both their hands without immediate medical attention. And whoever this was had lost all the above.

It was total overkill. To kill someone—and it wasn't as if Nathan planned on killing someone, but it paid to have some idea how to kill someone just in case it was ever necessary— there were a hell of a lot of easier ways to do it than *behead* them. Besides, it wasn't as though swords or axes or other traditional beheading tools were common in 2017 Vancouver.

Axes.

That thought sparked in Nathan's mind. The only people he'd seen who carried axes were the Huntsmen. And sure, they were metaphorical axes rather than literal axes—they were tattoos of an axe—but if the Huntsmen could get their hands on automatic weapons, an actual axe was hardly a stretch.

Nathan crept forward, careful to edge around the blood as much as possible. He should feel something, he knew: guilt, fear, horror. But curiosity fueled him and, for now, it had pushed aside everything else, even nausea, and replaced it with a much simpler need: to *know*.

Why behead a human? Why behead a human *and* take their hands? It didn't make sense. Real life wasn't an episode of *Dexter*. If you wanted to kill someone, there were a thousand easier ways.

Say what you wanted to kill wasn't human, though. Say it was superhuman. Supernatural.

Excitement bubbled in his chest as he neared the body. This was it. The proof he'd been looking for. Of course, it could be that the body was another werewolf—and that thought gave him a split second's pause—but after the shitshow earlier that year with GNAAW and the Huntsmen and Kiara's pack, it seemed highly unlikely that either organization would be active in the area without contacting Kiara first.

No, no way this was a werewolf. This had to be something else.

Nathan crouched down, as close to the body as he could get without disturbing the pool of blood around it. Without the head it was impossible to identify who it was. Whoever it was had been a guy, one who wore the same non-descript summer guy-clothes as Nathan: a plain T-shirt and shorts, with sneakered feet and white socks that contrasted starkly with the blood and the body's brown skin. Beyond that, it could be anyone.

Any*thing*.

Nathan's thoughts raced. Taking the head was easy; presumably that would kill most supernatural creatures. It would certainly be his first go-to. But the hands? That was new. *That was interesting. What about those hands had been a threat?*

He bent closer, chewing on his bottom lip as he studied the wounds.

The door to the recycling room opened. Nathan startled, nearly falling flat on his ass for the second time. The woman—Nathan recognized the willowy redhead from his building—took one look at Nathan, one look at the body at his feet, and began to scream.

Fuck.

Chapter Nine |

"THIS IS—" *NOT WHAT IT looks like.* Nathan didn't bother to finish his sentence. His neighbor backed rapidly out of the room; the door swung closed behind her. The door wasn't thick enough to provide much in the way of soundproofing, and his head ached from her raw shrieks.

The police would be here soon. If the woman—Elise? Emily?— wasn't calling them right now, surely another of the building's residents would. And Nathan was the only person in the room with a very dead body.

This could be bad. Real bad.

Nathan stood, wincing. His head swam; black dots appeared like flies in front of his vision. *Not good, not good.* The last thing he needed was to pass out. With his luck, he'd fall on top of the corpse. He glanced down at it again, thoughtlessly.

Dee, with her blond curls strewn in disarray, her dress torn, her collarbone gleaming wet and red.

Nathan jerked back. His pulse roared in his ears. He looked again, and the image of Dee was gone. The headless, handless corpse remained. Nathan's skin was clammy, and his fingers shook. He tried to flatten them against his thighs, but froze when he remembered the blood on them.

The flashback to his nightmare reminded him of one thing: Whoever was dead had been a who, not a what. They were someone's Dee, and he couldn't let his academic interest in what other magic might be out there gloss over that fact.

The screaming had finally stopped. He needed to get his shit together so he'd be able to talk to the cops. And, he hoped, not get arrested for murder.

Nathan washed his hands in his bathroom sink. He dried them hastily on the hand towel and picked up a bottle of Advil. He dumped three of the small white pills into his hand and carefully closed his fingers over them before he stepped naked into the running shower.

Nathan popped the pills into his mouth and kept it open as he moved directly into the spray. Hot water filled his mouth, and he swallowed. The heat made the pounding in his head worse, but he needed to wash off the blood before he could crawl into bed.

It was later now, hours past his planned afternoon nap. Since it was mid-July it'd be light out until nine o'clock or so, and, the way his exhaustion had doubled, he doubted he'd wake up even when the sun set.

The excitement he'd felt upon finding the body had faded. The hour he'd spent cooling his heels waiting to be questioned by the police, with no access to his phone—not that it would have mattered; the screen was damaged from being thrown onto the concrete—had been more than enough time for the thrill of possibly confirming the existence of supernatural creatures other than werewolves to be replaced by the monotony of a waiting room and the growing discomfort of blood drying against his clothes and bare skin.

Nathan turned to tip his head back under the spray. He grimaced. Pain flared again, as the hot water contacted the rather sizeable goose egg on the back of his head. There'd been a couple paramedics on scene—neither of whom had been Cole or one of the handful of Cole's work friends that Nathan knew. One of them had checked him out while he was waiting to speak to the detective and given Nathan the all-clear and an ice pack.

He'd been grateful for both and tempted to see if the paramedics could reach Cole, but, before he'd had a chance to ask, the detective had stepped into the building's commandeered party room, and the questions had begun.

He'd been spared having to go down to the station. His dramatic entrance into the garbage and recycling room was quite literally written in blood. And, as he hadn't been hiding a human head or pair of hands on his person, nor were they found in the same room as the body—and Nathan—he had been released after another hour spent repeating his story over and over, until the detective had determined he had nothing more to add. She'd released him, but cautioned him not to leave the country. He'd taken her card and promised to call if he thought of anything relevant.

Since he couldn't explain that he suspected whoever had died was a supernatural being of some sort, he doubted he'd be calling Detective Mira, or calling anyone, for that matter, until he got a new phone.

Nathan used a loofah to scrub off the more stubborn blood caked on his forearms. Until last year, he'd never had to wash off someone else's blood. Now he was doing it for the second time. He remembered the horror of the first time: standing shirtless in front of Dee's kitchen sink and frantically soaping his arms to his elbows while she showered in the bathroom. They hadn't known, then, if the two teenagers who'd been mauled by crywolf would survive the attack. Nathan had learned only hours earlier that werewolves actually existed.

He paused in his scrubbing. This was the second time he'd had to talk to the cops as well. Was he on some list somewhere? A person of interest? How many times could someone conceivably be a witness to violent attacks before the police started looking hard at that witness? He'd have to be careful, he realized. He'd have to keep his digging about the victim under the radar, because of course he was going to dig.

Ever since he'd learned about werewolves, about GNAAW, Nathan had several Google alerts set for certain keywords—*werewolves* and *GNAAW* were two of them. Nothing real or relevant had popped. Whoever scrubbed social media and the Internet of actual-werewolf-related content at GNAAW was doing a stellar job, much to Nathan's irritation. He'd had slightly better luck combing through the library archives at the university. Nothing explicitly confirmed the existence of humans who could transform into wolves at will, but there were hints, allusions. Suspicious blocks of text had been destroyed; certain volumes were missing. The absence of information was almost more telling than its presence.

Nathan squeezed the loofah and watched with detachment as pink-tinged water swirled into the drain.

He'd begin tomorrow with new criteria for his search. He finally had a specific direction to focus on. Scanning headlines for anything vaguely supernatural had yet to pay off. But now that he knew what to look for, he hoped he'd have better luck.

Hands. The hands may be the key he'd been missing. And his were finally clean, so, after one last rinse, Nathan shut off the water.

Sore body protesting, he stepped gingerly out of the shower. He'd be bruised to shit tomorrow, he suspected, and it would take a week or two before he'd be able to sit down without wincing. *Well.* It certainly wasn't his first or second time experiencing those side effects, though they were usually the result of a much more pleasant evening.

Nathan dried off quickly and wrapped his towel around his waist. He left the fan on in the bathroom to clear the steam and padded barefoot into the kitchen.

Cole stood at the island with his arms crossed over his chest.

"Jesus." Nathan pressed a hand to his chest to calm the frantic leap of his heart. "Are you trying to kill me?"

"Are *you* trying to kill *me?*" Cole was in his uniform, and his eyes were dark with anger. "Why didn't you call?" he asked, disapproval heavy in his voice.

"Why didn't I—?" Nathan broke off, frustrated. "I slipped in a pool of blood and broke my phone." He grabbed his phone off the kitchen counter and slapped it down on the island beside Cole to display the shattered screen. "And then I found a body. And then the police showed up. So I've been a little busy."

"I had to hear about it from a coworker, who caught the call over the scanner and recognized your address." Cole uncrossed his arms, the anger fading from his face until all that was left was concern. "Are you okay?"

"I'm fine."

Cole ignored him and moved closer to run his hands carefully over Nathan's body. Nathan rolled his eyes, but let Cole finish his inspection. He winced when Cole's fingers brushed lightly over the goose egg. Cole made a soft noise of sympathy in his throat and dropped a kiss onto Nathan's bare shoulder.

"I wish I'd been there. I wish we'd gotten the call."

"Me too. Then you could have had a look at the body." Now that Cole was here, Nathan's enthusiasm kicked up, temporarily displacing his exhaustion. "I'm pretty sure, whoever died, I don't think they were human. Or not fully, anyway."

"What?" Cole didn't draw back, but his body tensed. "What do you mean?"

"I think this is the proof I've been looking for. That werewolves aren't the only supernatural thing that's real."

"Nathan…"

"Someone cut off that guy's head *and* his hands. Who does that! Why go through all that effort to kill a regular person when there are, like, a zillion easier ways to do it?"

Cole sighed. "We've been over this. There aren't other supernatural beings."

"And there used to not be *any* supernatural beings. Now there are werewolves." Nathan huffed out a breath. "I don't know why you're so dead set against the idea that if werewolves are real, why can't, like, vampires be real too."

"Just because every paranormal romance novel written in the last twenty years has werewolves and vampires doesn't mean that the real world does."

"Or it means exactly that. I mean, maybe not vampires, but pop culture is full of references to other mythical creatures. History is full of references. There has to be some truth to that."

"Sometimes stories are just stories."

"And *sometimes* they aren't." Nathan jabbed a pointed finger at Cole's chest. "Case in point. So it stands to reason that other stuff might not be just stories as well."

"Except that we would know about other things." Cole said, his *we* meaning werewolves. "And we don't."

"That's what you keep saying."

"I'm not lying to you. Why would I?" Hurt, Cole stepped back.

"I don't know." Nathan gave a jerky shrug. "Maybe you aren't. Maybe you don't know. Maybe GNAAW is hiding it, like they hid the Huntsmen."

"The Huntsmen weren't hidden. They were… there were enough rumors. The specific details were on a need-to-know basis."

"Kiara called them a myth." Nathan squared his shoulders. "There are an awful lot of myths—and most of them have a lot more literature to back them up than the Huntsmen."

Cole scrubbed a hand through his beard. "You just discovered a body and were questioned by the police, on top of sustaining a head injury. Why don't we get you to bed and we can talk about this more tomorrow if you'd like?"

"Don't do that."

"Do what?"

"Patronize me like that, like you're worried about me."

"I *am* worried about you."

"But not like you're worried about me because of what happened tonight. Like you're *worried about me*. Like I'm losing it. I'm not losing it! Someone just had their head and their hands removed—probably to ensure they actually died and stayed dead. Tell me that doesn't seem strange to you?"

Cole lifted his own hands in a placating gesture. "Yes, okay? That is weird. But weird doesn't automatically translate to supernatural."

"It does in my life," Nathan said.

Cole closed his eyes. "I'm sorry for that."

"I'm not," Nathan emphasized. "I want to know what else is out there. I want to know all the other things inhabiting this planet that are supposed to be made up."

"There aren't any others, though, Nathan. It's just us. Just werewolves."

"No." Nathan shook his head. "I don't accept that."

"It's not going to change whether you accept it or not; it's the truth."

"And a year ago, *werewolves weren't real*. That was my truth."

Cole exhaled slowly through his nostrils. "I understand—"

"No! You don't! You can't!" The sudden edge to his voice bordered on hysterical, and Nathan fought to tone it down. No one listened to hysterical people, and Nathan knew he wasn't hysterical. He *was* onto something. "You don't know what it's like to have your world turned upside down like mine has been. I know you're trying, and I appreciate that, but you don't know. So please, don't tell me to stop trying to figure this out."

"There isn't anything to figure out." Cole gripped Nathan's arm. "Someone killed a guy in your building. It's shitty, and unfair, and seriously alarming. You should never have had to see something like that. But I'm worried." He ignored Nathan's flinch and tightened his grip to prevent Nathan from pulling away. "I'm worried about you. You aren't sleeping and, when you do, you have nightmares. Finding a body is hard enough, let alone a brutally murdered body. It stands to reason that you'd be trying to make sense of what happened, and, given everything that you and Deanna have had to deal with in the last year, I get why you'd think this might be supernatural in origin. Listen to me, though, when I tell you that it isn't. There aren't any more mythological beings out there. There's just you and me. That's it. I promise." There was zero guile in Cole's earnest expression; his worried eyes held nothing but care.

Nathan bit his tongue and told himself that now wasn't the time to keep pushing. He and Cole had had this same conversation more than once since Nathan had stood helplessly in a moonlit and blood-soaked clearing a year ago and witnessed a wolf transform into the handsome, bearded guy who now stood in front of him.

"I think you're wrong," he said finally. "I don't want to fight about it. I just think you're wrong."

Cole dropped his hand. "I'm not trying to fight you."

Nathan twisted past Cole, careful to maintain the distance between them. "I need to sleep. I'm going to bed."

"Would you like me to stay here tonight?"

Nathan blinked away a sudden onslaught of tears, the kindness in Cole's offer nearly undoing him. "Yes. Please."

"I love you."

"I know."

Nathan felt the weight of that love as he climbed the stairs. The thread between him and Cole became more taut with each fight, each argument aborted a minute too late. Whether that taut thread would stretch or break, he wasn't sure.

Chapter Ten |

"WHAT IS GOING ON?" JAMIE asked the second Cole answered his phone.

Cole sighed heavily into the receiver and sat up on Nathan's couch. Though Nathan had showered, and Cole had tossed Nathan's clothes in the laundry, the scent of stale blood lingered in the apartment. It made Cole's skin prickly.

"I've got nearly twenty texts from Dee about Nathan finding a body? One that he's saying isn't human…"

Cole marked his page and set his book down on the coffee table. He'd overheard Nathan typing on his laptop before turning in. He supposed he should have expected Nathan to talk to Deanna—and he should have offered to let Nathan call her using Cole's phone. But he'd been distracted: concerned for Nathan and anxious about the growing tension between them, exacerbated no doubt by the argument they'd just had.

"He was taking out the recycling, and there was a body. A decapitated body."

"Holy shit." Jamie's empathy was instant and sincere.

"Yeah." Cole rubbed the bridge of his nose. "The hands were missing too. It wasn't pretty." When he'd arrived at Nathan's building, the police had been swarming over the scene. Cole's paramedic uniform and ID had gotten him past the police tape. He hadn't gone into the recycling room—he'd been stopped at the door—but he'd seen and smelled the carnage. "Because of that—the head and the hands—Nathan thinks it must be supernatural."

Jamie sighed. He concentrated and could hear Arthur's gentle snores—presumably as he curled up on the couch beside Jamie. Deanna had long ago given up on enforcing her no-dogs-on-the-couch rule. Cole closed his eyes and leaned back. If he focused hard enough, he could almost convince himself that he sat there beside her, that the couch against his back wasn't Nathan's black leather, skin-warm in the summer heat, but the more forgiving teal-colored cloth of Jamie's.

"He's still not sleeping, hey?"

"No." Cole glanced up at the apartment's loft bedroom. "Well, not at night, anyway." He couldn't see Nathan, but the steady beat of his heart and the rhythm of his breathing told him Nathan had finally passed out. This far into July there were still a lot daylight hours left, and Cole hoped Nathan slept through every one of them.

"Pale skin, hollow eyes, only sleeps during the day... Maybe he's a vampire."

"Ha, ha. That would almost be funny, if we hadn't just had another fight about whether or not vampires are real."

"Vampires? Seriously?"

"Not vampires specifically, but anything other than us."

"Aw, shit. I'm sorry."

"It's okay." It was Cole's turn to sigh. "He's in shock right now, though who knows whether he'll acknowledge that or not. He still thinks I'm lying or that GNAAW is lying. I don't know what else to do. How do you prove something doesn't exist?"

With no helpful answer, Jamie stayed silent. Cole wished he was actually in the same room with his cousin.

"Do you ever worry—" The words were out of his mouth before he'd realized he meant to speak them.

"That we should never have involved them?" Jamie finished his question. "Yeah." Fabric rustled on Jamie's end of the line. He pictured her leaning forward, her elbows on her knees, her honey-gold eyes intent and serious. "I thought about that a lot, after the Huntsmen."

Deanna had been held at gunpoint, trapped in an alleyway with Kiara and Jamie and Ryn, and, unlike the others, without any supernatural defenses. Cole hadn't been there, but days later he had seen Nathan slumped in a chair with an angry bruise on his cheek being used as bait. He understood Jamie's helpless fury.

"And?" he prompted.

"Yeah, I worry. But I've gone over it and over it, and I don't believe I could have done anything differently. When crywolf was after Deanna because of her work at *Wolf's Run* she was in real danger. And she didn't realize it." Jamie gave a humourless laugh. "Because werewolves aren't real. So how could she take threats from someone claiming to be one seriously? I had to tell her. I had to keep her safe. I couldn't have known… I don't know. I don't know if this is better. I don't know if I could have found another way to stop crywolf. I was in love with her already. I would have had to tell her, at some point, or leave her. And on one hand… I'm almost grateful for him. I know how that sounds. But because I *had* to tell her, I didn't have to decide."

"Right." Cole understood. There'd been no need to come out, as it were, to Nathan. No need to decide if the truth about what Cole was would be well met or whether it was a truth worth sharing. Nathan had been introduced to the pack's world in the worst way and had witnessed werewolves at their most monstrous. It was a wonder, really, that Nathan hadn't run screaming, that he trusted the werewolves as much as he did—if not in everything, in most things.

"You know GNAAW has a dating app now?" Jamie asked suddenly.

"What? Really?"

"Yeah. I think probably to prevent this sort of thing."

"Go figure." He wondered what they called it. *Growlr? Heat?* On second thought, maybe he didn't want to know.

"Anyway, I just wanted to check in."

"Thanks. He'll be all right. He just needs time."

"Check in on *both* of you. I know this hasn't been easy on you either."

Cole shifted uncomfortably on the couch. "I'm fine."

"It's okay if you're not," Jamie reminded him gently. "You don't always have to be, you know."

"If one of us doesn't keep a level head, who will?" It was half in jest. Between his stormy sister and now Alpha, Kiara; her reckless lover, their new packmate Ryn; and daydreaming Jamie, Cole figured someone had to keep them all on track. "But I appreciate it." He headed her off. "I am okay, though. And he'll be okay." Cole had to believe in that, if nothing else.

"All right. I love you. Dee and I are here if you need anything."

"Thank you."

"And tell Nathan I'm sorry he had to see that."

"Will do."

Jamie ended the call, and Cole dropped his phone on the coffee table. Unperturbed, Nathan continued to sleep upstairs. Restless now, Cole stood.

He *was* fine, he reasoned as he made his way into the kitchen. He'd known the risks of dating a human. Besides, as Nathan had pointed out, he wasn't the one who had to deal with reality being turned upside down. It wasn't surprising that Nathan was struggling with it, and maybe, Cole needed to be more understanding.

The fridge was appallingly empty. Out of all of them, Nathan was the one who cooked with the most confidence, so seeing nothing but three bottles of beer, two wizened apples, and an empty pizza box was disheartening.

With Nathan sleeping, Cole could do little to help—but he could pick up groceries—the bare minimum, at least.

Cole cocked his head and listened for Nathan's slow, even breaths. He slept deeply enough that Cole figured he had more than enough time to get to the grocery store and back before Nathan woke. But just in case…

He found the pad of paper Nathan kept in the drawer with all the takeout menus and, after a frustrating minute of searching, a pen as well.

Gone for groceries. Back soon.

He hesitated, wanting to say more, but not sure what else there was.

I love you.

It was all the certainty he had to offer and it would have to be enough.

Chapter Eleven |

ARE YOU STILL AT WORK?

Nathan glanced at his phone to see the text from Cole. He'd refused to miss any work, despite Cole's not-so-subtle hints that maybe Nathan could use a sick day or two. It had been five days now since he'd found the body, long enough for it to have been identified, and for the information to have made its way to the media.

GRUESOME MURDER IN MOUNT PLEASANT APARTMENT screamed the headline on the computer screen in front of Nathan.

Police have released the identity of the man found beheaded in a Mount Pleasant apartment building over the weekend. Jag Gilbert, 32, was an accountant with…

Nathan's mouse hovered over the x button on the browser tab. He'd read the article so many times he'd lost track—he could recite it, word for word, though it hadn't given him any new information. Once the police had identified the body, they'd interviewed Nathan a second time. Jag Gilbert had lived in Nathan's building—a floor above.

Nathan hadn't recognized the name when Detective Mira had asked. He had recognized the photo she'd shown him. He saw the flashing smile of the Indian guy he recognized when they passed each other in the hallway or made small talk about the weather with in the elevator— the one who'd scared the crap out of him the other night on the roof.

It was weird to think that neither of them had asked each other's name. Like Nathan, Jag had probably assumed there was no rush; there was plenty of time for casual acquaintances to become friends. *Would they have been friends, eventually? Had they had common interests?*

Nathan suspected one, at least.

As though summoned, his phone lit with another text.

Are you still coming over for dinner?

Nathan groaned. He'd agreed yesterday to dinner at Cole's apartment, with Kiara and probably Ryn as well.

You know you don't have to if you don't want to.

Great, now he felt bad about his groan. He groaned again, doubling the guilt, and picked up his phone.

Yeah, I'm coming. It wasn't as if he had a choice. He thought Cole had probably invented the whole "kill them with kindness" concept. Sure, he could have said no, but then Cole would have been understanding, and then Nathan would think *he* was the monster. **Do you need me to grab anything?**

He finally closed his browser tabs and half-heartedly skimmed his work email before he signed out. He saw nothing urgent, nothing that couldn't wait until tomorrow.

Kiara says buns, if you want garlic toast.

On it.

He grabbed his messenger bag and headed out.

"Look, I'm not saying *House of Cards* Robin Wright isn't a complete babe, I'm saying *Wonder Woman* Robin Wright would go toe-to-toe with you in a way no one else could. She's an Amazon."

"Hmm." Ryn toyed with the ends of their hair. "I'm still going with Madam President Claire Underwood. Remember that powder-blue power dress she wore in the season finale?" They shuddered with exaggerated arousal.

Kiara spread butter irritably, which, until now, Nathan would have sworn was impossible to do.

"But an *Amazon*," Kiara belabored.

"I have to agree with Ryn," Nathan inserted. He didn't—he thought both Robin Wrights were equally dreamy, but disagreeing with Kiara would drive her insane, and he liked doing that. He took an innocent sip of his beer as she shot him a glare.

"I don't understand you two," she muttered, adding garlic. "It's like you don't have eyes. Or brains." She picked up her plate of garlic toast and marched out to the balcony where Cole manned the barbecue.

Nathan waited until she was out of the room before he broke, snickering. "You'd think it would get old," he said to Ryn.

"It never does," they replied with relish. "She's just too easy to tease."

"I can hear you!" Kiara yelled from the balcony.

Right. Werewolf hearing. Nathan made a face. "Can't hear that," he muttered.

Kiara stuck her head around the sliding glass doors and narrowed her eyes. Nathan blew her a kiss.

He used to think he'd get tired of being so easily overheard. It kind of killed any expectation of privacy—but the pack was courteous about that sort of thing. Cole had told him that one of the first lessons taught young wolves was to expect that they would hear or smell—and Nathan didn't want to know anything more about *that*—things that they weren't meant to, and that it was not only polite, but necessary, to ignore them. He imagined that growing up in a household of other werewolves, as Cole, Kiara, and Jamie had, would hammer in that lesson.

Ryn on the other hand... He looked at them with interest. "When did your super hearing kick in?"

They hummed. "Just before my first shift. I was twelve, maybe? Overheard my teacher complaining about all the ESL students in our class." They grinned. "So, I filled all the drawers in her desk with shaving cream."

Nathan tried to picture a preteen Ryn with fierce dark eyes and a sullen smirk. "She catch you?"

"Nope. I kept it up for the rest of the school year. No discernable pattern, not even the same kind of shaving cream twice." Ryn grinned at the memory. "She got locks on all the drawers after the second time, and that was when I discovered my strength." They flexed their biceps demonstratively. "And on the last day of class I used cooked rice. Do you know how hard it is to get rice out of something once it's all gummed up and gross?" Ryn asked with relish.

"Where'd you get that much rice?" Cole's voice floated through the balcony doors.

"I'm Korean. That's like asking a white person where they get brunch."

Nathan choked on his mouthful of beer. Ryn pounded him on the back.

"Thanks," he said, once he'd finished coughing, and took another swig of beer to soothe his now-raw throat.

"No problem. I'll pound you any time." Ryn caught Nathan's eyes, and there was enough of a teasing suggestion in her gaze that Nathan's pulse jumped.

"Keep it in your pants," Kiara growled, coming back into the kitchen.

Nathan cleared his throat. Ryn just laughed.

Though Ryn was a match for Nathan as far as flirtation went, he was fairly certain that they and Kiara were monogamous. No matter what Ryn implied, there was not likely to be any pegging in his future—with Ryn, anyway. Probably.

Ryn winked.

As though Kiara could sense the direction of Nathan's thoughts, she poked him in the side. "Quit fantasizing about my lover."

"I'm not." Only a little. "They started it."

"Baby, you know I can't help myself around a pretty face." Ryn rose from the table and swept Kiara into their arms. Kiara yelped and pretended to struggle—despite her smaller size, her strength outmatched Ryn's—before she gave in and tilted her face for Ryn to kiss with enough enthusiasm that Nathan wondered if he should join Cole on the balcony.

When the two finally broke apart, Kiara's sharp eyes had gone soft, and Ryn tangled their fingers, keeping Kiara tucked to their side.

Nathan saw Cole watching from the doorway; his eyes crinkled as he smiled at his sister and her lover. There was a sudden pang in Nathan's chest: love for the man in front of him so strong that Nathan's throat tightened and his heart ached with it.

His life hadn't been easier since the Big Reveal, as he'd come to think of the whole werewolves-exist-thing, but he couldn't deny that finding Cole—or Cole finding him; he still wasn't sure how that worked—was the best thing that had ever happened to him. Even if they were so often at odds lately.

Nathan swallowed, dropped his gaze to his bottle of beer, and toyed with the label. He didn't want to be at odds with Cole. But he didn't understand why no one else seemed to be curious, why no one else wanted to entertain the possibility that there were other magical beings.

"Nathan." Cole's voice jerked Nathan out of his introspection. "I'm going to put yours on first, if that's okay?"

Nathan nodded. "Yeah, thanks."

"How come Nathan gets his first?" Ryn protested.

"So he doesn't get any meat on his tofu," Cole answered before Nathan could.

"Right. Vegetarian. I always forget."

Nathan raised an eyebrow.

Ryn shrugged. "You just don't seem the type is all." They patted Kiara on the butt and sat beside Nathan. "Why are you, anyway?"

Nathan looked away, not wanting to get into it when they'd avoided the topic so far. "If werewolves are real—"

"*If?*"

"If *werewolves* are real," he continued with dignity, "who's to say were-other-things aren't? Werecows. Werepigs. Werechickens." He shuddered. "Do you know how much bacon I used to eat? That's a brunch staple. And what if I ate…" He couldn't finish the thought. Three weeks after the showdown with crywolf, Nathan had been making his way through a burger when the possibility of other shapeshifters crossed his mind. He hadn't been able to eat meat since.

Ryn looked thoughtful. "Well." Their teeth flashed white. "I guess it's a good thing that I'm an apex werepredator."

"Ryn!"

Chapter Twelve |

"ARE YOU ALL RIGHT IF I stay?"

Dinner long over, Nathan and Cole sat on the balcony and watched the sun set over False Creek. Nathan's bare feet were in Cole's lap; Cole's strong fingers pressed deftly into the arch of Nathan's right foot as Nathan bit back a groan of pleasure.

"Of course." Cole sounded surprised that Nathan would think otherwise. Kiara and Ryn had left an hour ago. Kiara'd said something about binging *Wynonna Earp* while Ryn mouthed "sex" behind her back.

"Thanks." Nathan slid lower in his chair and let his eyes fall closed as Cole switched feet. He couldn't remember the last time he'd felt so relaxed. Not since he'd found the body, for sure.

The heat of the day had ebbed; the air was now pleasantly warm as opposed to sweltering. With his stomach full of delicious food, a cold beer dangling from his fingertips, and his handsome lover humming quietly along to Snow Patrol as he massaged Nathan's feet, Nathan never wanted to be anywhere else.

If he could keep this moment, hold it safe and perfect and untouched, he would. All he needed was a Pensieve. And if werewolves were real, who's to say the world of Harry Potter wasn't?

He cracked open an eye to look at Cole, who was gazing serenely at the water. Nathan wished... He wasn't sure what he wished for: to not be so inquisitive, to take Cole and Kiara at their word that there was nothing else out there, to be able to let this go.

He couldn't, though; he knew that. And there was no sense wishing he was otherwise. He could keep it to himself tonight, that much he could offer.

"Cole."

Cole turned his focus back to Nathan. Their eyes met, and Nathan drew in a breath. In the soft light of the late evening and the glow of the balcony lights, Dee had helped Kiara string earlier in the summer, Cole's eyes were golden. They shone like good scotch, heady, needing to be parceled out in small doses, lest it leave a person overwhelmed, dizzy, breathless. Nathan wanted to pour himself the full bottle, to drink it straight from the source.

He pulled his feet from Cole's lap and leaned forward; Cole came to meet him halfway. As their lips met, Nathan cupped Cole's face. Cole's beard was coarse against his hands as his lips parted softly against Nathan's.

The dual sensations spun lazily through Nathan: rough and soft, giving and firm. He buried his fingers in Cole's thick hair, tilted his head, and deepened the angle of the kiss. Cole shuddered; his hands flexed against Nathan's back as he drew him closer.

Need was there, slow and rolling, and Nathan gave in to unhurried pleasure. He eased his tongue into Cole's mouth; his entire body lit up when Cole's tongue tangled with his. Cole tasted of the mango sherbet Ryn had brought for dessert.

Cole's hands skimmed under the hem of Nathan's shirt, then lifted it to bare his back. The slight breeze ghosted over Nathan's skin; Cole's fingers trailed in its wake. Not breaking the kiss, Nathan closed the distance between them and straddled Cole's lap.

He hissed out a breath when Cole rocked his hips up; Cole's hardening cock tented the thin fabric of his board shorts. Nathan slid a hand down from Cole's hair and pressed the flat of it firm against Cole's chest. Cole groaned against Nathan's mouth; his hands moved to knead Nathan's ass and pull him closer.

Through his shirt, Nathan drew a thumb across Cole's nipple, circled till it hardened. Cole broke the kiss with a gasp; his head fell back against the chair. Nathan ran his lips over Cole's bared throat and nipped lightly at the skin.

"You know," he murmured as he found Cole's other nipple, already hard, with his other hand, "you do have one thing that separates you from all my other lovers."

"Just one?" A laugh rumbled in Cole's chest.

"Mmhmm. With that super-human healing of yours…" Nathan swirled his tongue over the side of Cole's neck and then bit down and sucked firmly. Cole went taut under him; his fingers dug into Nathan's ass as he ground Nathan down against him.

"I never have to worry about leaving hickies," Nathan finished. He pulled back, watched the purpled skin fade to red, then vanish as though nothing had happened. He met Cole's eyes, grinned, and bent to bite another into Cole's neck.

Cole splayed his hands across Nathan's thighs; his fingers trembled as he fought not to leave his own bruises. Nathan loved the way Cole fell apart under him—all that strength and control gone graceless.

Cole hitched Nathan's hips closer, and Nathan obliged, rubbing himself over Cole's hard length. He wished he'd thought to change before dinner—what was the point in having a drawer at his boyfriend's if he didn't use it?—because the tight fit of his khakis had never been more apparent or uncomfortable.

Nathan grabbed Cole's shirt and pushed it up, gathering the fabric under Cole's armpits and baring his chest. Nathan leaned back, trusting Cole to hold him steady as he ran his hands through the forest of hair on Cole's chest. His chest hair was dark enough brown to be almost black and flecked with gray like Cole's beard. Nathan dragged his fingernails down and watched as the curls parted and sprang back.

"We could, uh, maybe go inside?" Cole suggested breathlessly when Nathan bent to pull one of Cole's nipples into his mouth. Nathan teased the sensitive flesh with his tongue, grinning when Cole jerked and swore.

"You were all about public displays of affection the other night," Nathan remarked. He glanced up to see Cole blush beneath his beard, and, entirely charmed, darted forward to steal another kiss.

"Smart ass," Cole murmured when Nathan relinquished his mouth. Nathan took a handful of the hair on one of Cole's pecs and tugged. Cole arched into it, even as he gripped Nathan's wrist to hold his hand still.

"Do you want to fuck me?" Cole asked, his voice gone low and smoky.

Nathan's mouth dried. "Yeah." He rubbed his thumb across Cole's kiss-swollen lower lip, then dipped it into Cole's mouth to feel Cole's lips close around it and suck. Nathan bit back a whimper.

Cole released Nathan's thumb. "Inside."

Nathan scrambled off Cole's lap, followed the older man through to the bedroom, and kicked the door closed behind them. It was unlikely that Kiara would come back tonight, but the one time she had waltzed into the apartment while Cole'd had Nathan in a… somewhat compromising position, had imprinted the importance of closing the door in Nathan's mind.

Cole yanked off his shirt, and Nathan hopped awkwardly as he tried to pull off his socks and walk toward the bed at the same time. He nearly toppled into the dresser, but Cole's hand shot out to catch him. Nathan swayed into Cole's steady embrace, kissing him messily as he struggled with the button on his pants. Cole laughed against Nathan's lips and swatted his hands away, undid Nathan's pants before Nathan could blink, and pushed him back toward the bed.

Nathan tripped over the pants that fell down his hips and landed face first on the mattress with an "Oof."

"Shit, are you—"

"Fine," Nathan huffed, already wriggling around to kick off the offending article of clothing, and pushed his briefs down with it. He sat up and pulled off his shirt as Cole stepped out of his shorts. He had not been, Nathan noted, wearing any underwear. "C'mere."

Cole obeyed without hesitation, crawling onto the bed and bracketing Nathan with his muscular arms. Nathan grinned and twisted his neck to bite at the inside of Cole's wrist. Cole growled, low, wolfish, and slid down Nathan's body.

Nathan went lax when Cole closed his mouth around Nathan's cock; the wet heat chased every other thought from his brain. Cole shouldered Nathan's legs apart so he could settle between them and took Nathan as far into his throat as he could.

Nathan didn't stop the moan that fell from his lips; he closed his eyes and gripped the bedsheets, which were new and moss green. Cole growled again, this time around Nathan's cock, and Nathan forgot the sheets and saw stars.

"Stop, stop," he begged, even as his hips bucked up into Cole. "I won't—I'm not gonna—I want to fuck you."

Cole came off him with an audible pop. "Yeah," he agreed, his voice rough and his lips slick. Panting, Nathan scrambled across the bed to the bedside table to grab the lube with shaking fingers.

When he turned back, Cole had obligingly rolled onto his front with his legs spread wide. His back was dusted with the same soft curls as his front, darker at his ass and across his thick thighs. Nathan gripped the base of his cock, taking a minute and a deep breath to slow himself down. He wanted to savor every moment with the gorgeous man splayed in front of him.

"You're beautiful." The words spilled from him. "I wish I was a photographer. I wish I could capture how you look right now, so I could show it to you. I'd make giant prints. I'd poster my walls with them."

Those whiskey-eyes full of unbanked heat, Cole turned his head to look at Nathan. Nathan let out a shuddering breath and went to him.

Nathan set the lube on the bed beside Cole. He'd get to that later. Cole's bare skin was warm under his palm; he felt soft hair over hard muscle. He eased down onto his side and stroked his hand over Cole, from the nape of his neck to the curve of his ass. Cole melted under the touch and buried his head into his arms as Nathan ran his hand over the expanse of Cole's back, down the round globe of his ass, across his muscular thigh.

He rolled on top of Cole, covered the length of Cole's naked body with his own. Cole inhaled sharply as Nathan's weight settled on top of him, and Nathan found Cole's hands, gripped them tight.

The sensation of Cole's body under his, of all that strength and power laid out for his exploration, raced like a drug through Nathan's veins. He dropped his head and nosed into the dip of Cole's neck, breathing in the spice of Cole's body wash. Cole made a noise low in his throat; his hips moved as he searched for friction against the sheets.

Nathan laughed softly, running his hands down Cole's arms before reluctantly lifting himself up so he could move down the bed.

As Cole had settled earlier between Nathan's legs, Nathan now settled between Cole's. He breathed lightly across Cole's ass and watched the delicate hair tremble and Cole's hips jerk. Anticipation closed Nathan's throat as he parted Cole's cheeks.

"Can I?" he asked.

Cole's response was muffled. "God, yes."

Nathan swept his tongue over Cole's dusky hole. He usually gave Cole a second or two to adjust, knowing how sensitive the werewolf was, but now he refused. He tongued Cole's rim. Breath panting hot, wet saliva making a mess of them both, he delved in and pushed against the puckered skin. Cole cried out; his thighs tensed as he fought to hold himself still while Nathan plundered.

It wasn't until Cole writhed, breathless and increasingly desperate, that Nathan pulled back.

"Fuck me. Now," Cole demanded.

With his cock hanging heavy between his legs, so hard it ached, Nathan readily agreed. He grabbed the lube, flipped open the cap, and poured a generous amount onto Cole's ass, watching as it slid down over Cole's flushed hole while he coated his fingers.

Cole groaned when Nathan sank the first finger into him. Cole's body was hot and tight, soft as velvet. Nathan moved slowly, working his finger in and out of Cole until he could add a second. Cole let out a sharp, hissing breath when Nathan twisted and his fingers brushed just right.

"I can take it," Cole insisted, his ass rising to meet Nathan's gentle thrusts.

"Not yet." Nathan continued to press his two fingers into Cole; he waited until they moved easily. He added a third with a bit more effort. Cole nearly arched off the bed when Nathan pumped all three.

Nathan's heart fluttered in his throat; desire burned across his skin. Whatever it was between him and Cole—love, lust, longing— it expressed itself in contradictions. It was enough to drive a saner man than him insane—hard and soft, a burn and a balm. His fingers trembled as he withdrew and reached again for the lube.

Cole rose to his knees and watched Nathan with eyes gone the slate gray of wolves.

When Nathan closed a slick hand around himself, he bit back a groan. He used condoms, religiously, with his other lovers, but Cole's werewolf constitution meant he could neither catch nor pass on STIs. It had taken no small amount of persuasion on Cole's part to assure Nathan he wouldn't be putting anyone else at risk. It wasn't *better* without, but it was different. Nathan steadied himself at Cole's entrance. "Ready?"

"More than," was Cole's impatient response. *Well then.* Nathan thrust forward, burying himself to the hilt, and his curse was echoed by Cole.

Cole rocked forward on his knees only to push back before Nathan could catch his breath. Nathan swore again; his hands gripped Cole's waist. Cole grunted, less with the effort and more with the sensation, as he rocked again.

"Jesus, just—let me breathe!" Nathan managed. Pleasure bolted like lightning through his bones.

"No." Cole's breathless voice held the edge of a laugh. Nathan growled in frustration, firmed his grip on Cole's hips, and met Cole thrust for thrust.

His focus narrowed to the slap of skin against skin, the sharp jolts of pleasure, which lengthened each time he sank into Cole. Time dissolved into an endless spiral. Hand still slick with lube, Nathan gripped Cole in his fist and pumped. Cole cried out and then stilled, finally allowing Nathan to control the pace.

Heat pooled in Nathan's stomach as his orgasm began to build. Cole's cock pulsed in his hand.

Cole snarled as he came in sudden, liquid bursts over Nathan's fist. His entire body clenched, and Nathan gritted his teeth; the intensity was nearly too much for him to bear. He fought to hold off, to stay balanced on the knife-edge of too-much and not-enough and *almost*. If he could be here forever, slamming into Cole and out again, his hand coated in Cole's hot, wet come, he'd chose it. He'd take it over any other future, any other reality.

His orgasm ripped through him, sudden and blinding. Nathan rode it out, hard and urgent until he'd wrung out every last ounce of pleasure and the sensations became too much. He collapsed on top of Cole, knowing that the werewolf could take his weight.

Cole sighed contentedly under Nathan. Sweat slicked their skin together, sweat and come. It should have been gross, but it wasn't. Nathan wanted every part of Cole—the sweet and the sticky.

You're the only person preventing that, the sly voice in his head intruded. *You only need to let this nonsense about other creatures go.*

Nathan burrowed his face into the bend of Cole's neck and pressed himself tighter. He wasn't going to let anything go, not his belief that something else was out there, not Cole. He could have both; he knew he could.

Maybe the answer was only to be more careful about his search.

As his heartbeat slowed and his ragged breathing smoothed, Nathan pushed away everything else but the man in bed with him.

Chapter Thirteen |

Nathan dug his pen into the page with more force than necessary. His boss Malaya's voice was a distant buzz at this staff meeting late in the afternoon on a Friday, a gloriously sunny summer Friday at that, and his focus was approximately zilch.

It didn't help that simply being in this particular meeting room made his skin itch and the side of his face throb with remembered pain. Today at least he'd been prepared for the reaction and had managed to avoid sitting in the seat where the Huntsmen had held him. He wasn't sure if sitting across from it was much better, though.

Stupid, he told himself, adding another line to his doodle. It wasn't as though anything that bad had happened here. It hadn't been good by any means, but Nathan and the wolves had all survived the showdown with the Huntsmen relatively unharmed.

His gaze moved up, unerring, to the ceiling. There was no discernable evidence that a bullet had plowed through that spot. It was as smooth and beige-colored as the rest of the room. That was no surprise. The Huntsmen worked to conceal both the existence of werewolves, and therefore the existence of themselves, from the rest of humanity. Cleaning up would have to be their forte.

He dropped his eyes to the pad of paper in front of him, which was angled toward his chest to hide that he wasn't taking notes. The doodle had begun as nothing, abstract lines and loops, but had since taken on shape: a hand.

There'd been no new information online about Jag's murder. If the police had found his head or his hands, they hadn't informed the public. Nathan hated being on the outside of the investigation. After a year of being a part of the inner circle of *werewolves are real*, it rankled to be a civilian again.

That wasn't the cops' fault; they didn't know that supernatural beings were alive and well in modern-day Canada. If Nathan could figure out what they knew somehow, then maybe he'd have an easier time trying to connect the dots on his end.

"Hey." He nudged Cris. She, a better employee than he, was actually taking notes. She glanced away from Malaya and raised her eyebrows. "You're decent with computers, right?" he asked in a whisper.

"We're kind of in the middle of something," she hissed back.

"No, I know, but—"

"Can't it wait like, twenty minutes?"

"I just wanna know if you could, like, hack into the police system. Or whatever."

"If I could—! Nathan."

"Can you?"

Malaya cleared her throat. "I know we're all eager to get to our weekends, but I do need you to focus." She looked pointedly at Nathan. He nodded vigorously, trying to keep the quick guilt off his face. Malaya waited a moment, then continued.

"I just need a yes or no," he said, lips barely moving.

"No! Do you know how hard that would be? I'm not Russia. And even if I could—which I can't—do you know what would happen if I got caught?" Cris shook her head. "Because I don't and I have no desire to find out."

Nathan sighed. It had been a long shot. *Maybe I could hire someone?* He worked at a university. It was full of kids who imagined themselves the next David Karp. But what if they did get caught, and told the police that Nathan had hired them? He'd probably go back to number-one murder suspect, since he couldn't explain that he needed to know what they knew so he could identify the supernatural being he was convinced Jag had been.

And that—that brought up a question Nathan hadn't given much thought. *Who had killed Jag?* He tapped his pen thoughtfully against his lips. There wasn't only one source of information about Jag, was there? Whoever killed him—whatever killed him—they knew what he was. All Nathan had to do was find the killer, and he'd get the answers he wanted.

On paper, the idea was ridiculous: Solve a murder the cops hadn't been able to solve yet. But Nathan was a step, more than one step, maybe five steps, ahead of them. He had access to information they didn't. He knew about an entire world that they didn't. So maybe he had to stop focusing on the regular world, the one the cops worked in, and start focusing on the other world.

He needed to talk to the Huntsmen.

Chapter Fourteen |

NATHAN DECLINED POST-MEETING DRINKS WITH Cris and a few of their other coworkers. He wasn't super proud of the lie—that he had plans with Cole—but since last year, lies about his personal life had become a necessity. And, he found, the more he lied, the easier it became, which wasn't really a surprise. As a queer kid from rural Redcliff, Alberta, he had learned to lie early. It was almost disconcerting how easily the skill came back.

"Have a good weekend!" He waved at Cris as he passed her office. She cocked a finger gun at him, and Nathan forced his fake smile wider until it seemed his face might crack.

Guns, real or otherwise, had joined the ever-lengthening list of things that sent a chill down his spine. He had no way to explain to Cris why. It was better to smile and nod and, if possible, to change the subject.

He jogged down the stairs, and pushed out into the sweltering summer afternoon. The university campus was never as crowded during the summer as it was the rest of the year, and he slowed his pace to appreciate the quiet of the main walkway. He felt a moment of indecision. It was a beautiful day, their regular on-campus pub would have a near-empty patio, and he could always meet his coworkers saying Cole got called into work. It would be easy to pretend his life was normal, just like theirs.

He snorted out a laugh at the naivety of the thought. Normal wasn't in his past, or his future. It was strange to think his discovery of his queerness, his identities as a pansexual, polyamorous man, were what made carrying the secret of werewolves seem almost natural. He'd done this before. He'd had huge chunks of his life that needed to be concealed. Moving to Vancouver had meant finally being able to take a breath of fresh air, to fully fill his lungs for the first time in his life. He'd felt free. It was past-tense, now, that freedom. The weight of another secret, the heaviness of knowing it was life-or-death, had settled over him.

He didn't regret it, Nathan assured himself as he turned off the main path toward the bus loop. He wouldn't trade knowing what he knew now for that feeling of freedom. He only wished he could have both.

That was neither here nor there, though, and lamenting what he couldn't have didn't help. He firmed his grip on his book bag and dismissed the part of him that yearned for a simple after-work beer. He had more important work to do.

Contacting the Huntsmen wouldn't be an easy task, and it wasn't as though he could phone Kiara and ask for her help. If she knew he was even *thinking* about reaching out to them, she'd probably skin him alive. Nathan wasn't sure if Cole would be able to save him. He didn't blame Kiara—after all, the Huntsmen had targeted her lover and the implication had been that they intended to kill Ryn, which was bad, or experiment on them, which was worse.

It was risky, he acknowledged. Dee was also liable to throw a fit if he mentioned it to her. But the pack was firmly under GNAAW's protection now. And Nathan was human. The Huntsmen would have no reason to go after him. Besides, he *would* be careful. He wasn't an idiot. He wasn't taking stupid risks just for the thrill of it. He knew what he was doing, even if he had to keep it quiet.

His phone buzzed against his leg as he settled into a seat at the back of the bus. Nathan fished it out of his pocket, and his face broke into a grin—real, this time, not forced—as he saw the message alert for his group chat with Isobel and Darren.

Isobel had sent a picture—a very explicit picture, featuring herself and her husband. The Black couple were entwined, Isobel's head was thrown back mid-laugh, and their skin shone with sweat. Nathan felt his cheeks go hot and glanced around to make sure that no one else had seen his screen.

I know you're having an ungodly week of hell, Isobel wrote, referring no doubt to the whole finding-a-murder-victim thing. **We were thinking of you last night though.**

Think about me more, please. Nathan responded, still grinning.

We were thinking it's been a while since you've come for dinner. Darren joined in. **Got any free time soon?**

Nathan's thumb hovered over the keyboard. He hadn't been avoiding Isobel and Darren per se. It was just that their date nights usually involved him staying the night at their condo in New Westminster. He hadn't seen them for almost two months now. He hadn't stayed the night with anyone other than Cole since he'd learned that, not only did he wake up screaming, but sometimes he talked in his sleep as well.

Out for drinks with coworkers. Nathan texted, the dovetailed lie came easily. **I'll check my calendar later and get back to you?**

Isobel's response was immediate. **Of course.**

And no pressure, Darren added. **We know you are busy!**

Saw those pics of you and Handsome Cole on fb ;) How is he???

He's out for drinks Isobel, Darren scolded. **Save it for in person!**

Sigh. Fine. But you'll give him a kiss for me, won't you, Nathan?

With tongue, Nathan promised. **Thanks for the check in. I'll get back to you soon! Miss you both.**

Darren sent a heart emoji.

Nathan closed the chat and slid his phone back into his pocket. He felt a fresh gladness in his chest. Isobel was a professor of philosophy.

He'd met her a few years ago when she'd taught a class at the university. He'd had an outrageous crush on her, and Dee had to suffer through several months of Nathan mooning over his unavailable, married work friend. Just as Nathan had begun to get a handle on his emotions and move them firmly into platonic admiration, Isobel had invited him for after-work drinks at the end of the semester and told him she'd be teaching full-time at one of Vancouver's other universities in the fall. Nathan had been crushed—for all of five minutes, until she'd wondered, now that she and Nathan wouldn't be working together, would he be interested in going to dinner with her and her husband? And that she and he were, by the way, non-monogamous. Nearly two years later, they were one of Nathan's longest relationships.

Nathan liked to date people who already had primary relationships. He enjoyed his freedom and his independence and knowing that he wasn't the center of someone else's world. He could flit in and out as it suited them all. That didn't mean that Isobel and Darren weren't deeply important to him; they were a significant part of his life, and he theirs.

Lighter than he'd been all day, Nathan got off at his stop and walked the block to his building. The garbage and recycling room was no longer blocked off, and Nathan hesitated at the door. It was closed, as it usually was. He thought about opening it, stepping through. Would he be greeted with by the stain of Jag's blood, or had the building manager been able to remove or cover it? Nathan's fingers brushed over the cool metal of the door handle, but he dropped his hand. He'd have to go in soon enough; his garbage bin was nearly full, but no sense rushing it.

He had more important things to focus on, such as how to get in touch with an underground group of professional werewolf hunters.

Chapter Fifteen .

COLE WOKE SLOWLY TO AN empty apartment. Kiara had stayed another night with Ryn, as evidenced by the silent absence of her breathing. Cole rolled onto his back from where he'd been curled around a pillow. He stretched against the sheets with eyes heavy-lidded against the sun that streamed through the bedroom's open window. He sank back into its warmth and wondered if it wouldn't be nice to slide back into sleep.

A Saturday off was rare, and he intended to enjoy it. He reached across the bed for his phone and smiled when he saw Nathan had finally returned his text. He swiped his thumb across the screen to read it.

Can't.

That was it, all Nathan had written. Cole's stomach twisted. He reread what he'd sent last night.

Hey, Happy Friday! I've got tomorrow off :) Any interest in going out to the lake with me?

Can't.

Cole dropped his phone onto the bedside table, sat up, and swung his feet to the cool hardwood floor. He tugged a frustrated hand roughly through his hair. He wasn't possessive—a person couldn't be possessive and date Nathan—but he was worried. And he was right to be, wasn't he? Nathan needed his space on occasion, and when that happened

Cole was more than happy to go on with his own life until Nathan wandered back into it. Nathan never stayed away long and was never cold or cruel about it. If Nathan needed space, Cole would give it unquestioningly. But Nathan was a fierce advocate for open and honest communication. In the past, he'd always been kind and clear when he'd wanted his own space.

"Can't" was certainly clear enough.

He sighed and let the exhale ripple through his body. Nathan was going through a lot right now—beyond what Cole could imagine, as Nathan had pointed out. If Nathan needed to be curt, Cole wouldn't hold that against him.

Naked and easy with that, Cole rose from the bed. The day was hot already. It would only get warmer, with the forecast predicting a sweltering twenty-eight degrees Celsius.

He picked up his phone and debated asking the pack if anyone wanted to go with him. They usually ran together or at least in pairs. Whether the desire for company was a wolf or a human one, Cole had never decided.

He shook his head. He'd take a page from Nathan's book and go on his own. Whoever he took was apt to ask after Nathan—not to nag or disapprove, but out of honest concern. Since Cole wasn't sure of the answer himself, he didn't think he'd like to hash it out with his family.

No worries, enjoy the sun! He replied to Nathan. Maybe he'd leave his phone at home, so he didn't spend the day itching to check on Nathan, who apparently wouldn't thank him for that.

It didn't take Cole long to get ready and within twenty minutes he was out the door and in the driver's seat of the car he and Kiara shared. With the windows rolled down and Halsey crooning through his speakers, Cole headed out of the city. Cat Lake was about an hour-and-a-half drive from Vancouver, just past Squamish. It was a favorite of Dee's and Nathan's, and the pack had quickly begun to appreciate the seclusion of the woods around it.

The last time, the whole pack plus Nathan had gone—and Arthur, of course. Cole and Jamie had commandeered the inflatable two-person raft and spent the afternoon drinking beer, eating chips, and reading in the middle of the lake. Kiara and Nathan had hiked in the surrounding woods. Ryn had almost gone with them, but Deanna had raced topless off the dock with Arthur a streak of gold beside her, and they'd landed in the lake with a giant splash that had Dee shrieking with laughter when she'd surfaced, looking like a freshwater mermaid. Ryn had shrugged, shucked off her shorts and tank top, and cannonballed after them in her sports bra and briefs.

It would be different to be on his own, Cole mused, as the city disappeared behind him and the road began to wind along the coast into Howe Sound. He tried to remember the last time he'd gone out alone and couldn't—not since he and Kiara had moved to the west coast, that was for sure.

The road spun lazily out before him. The sun gleamed off the water to his left; the mountains rose to his right. Cole enjoyed living in the city and its bustling humanity, but as he left it farther behind and the air that streamed through his open windows carried the scent of woods left to grow wild, an answering wildness stretched its limbs inside him. He was eager, suddenly, for a solo run through the woods.

Cole cranked up the music and let Vancouver and everyone in it drop away behind him.

THE GRAVEL PARKING LOT NEAR the lake was crowded, which wasn't unexpected. Cole edged his car between a minivan and a Jeep. He unlocked the trunk and pulled out a canvas backpack that had frayed rather seriously around the edges. He'd need a new one soon, he thought, as he'd thought every time this year he'd taken out the backpack. He'd been using the same one since his first shift, and it showed.

There was nothing special about the backpack, per se, but it had been a gift from his grandmother—his Alpha—before she'd passed. She'd put together backpacks for all of them, her children and her grandchildren and the wolves who weren't family through blood but through pack ties just as deep. She'd made a tradition that when a wolf first ran with the pack, they received a pack of their own. *Well, a* back*pack. But, still.* Cole was never sure if the pun was on purpose, or if a bag to stow your crap while you ran around on all fours was simply a matter of practicality.

Either way, he would be sorry to replace his. He fingered the straps of the bag as he swung it over his shoulder and settled the weight across his back before crossing the parking lot in the opposite direction of the people on their way to the lake.

A small, overgrown trail led into the woods. Cole pulled his baseball cap onto his head, slid on his sunglasses, and went in.

Chapter Sixteen |

It was cooler in the shade of the trees. As the noise of the parking lot and the lake-goers faded behind him, Cole relaxed his control.

He spent so much of his life in and around humans that he never felt stifled. It was second nature to keep his werewolf self hidden. But he couldn't deny the pleasure that flowed through him when he let go of the façade. It was like stepping from one world to the next. Humans held back so much of themselves. Theirs was a rigid existence, an adherence to rules and norms—not all of them, of course, and most people seemed happy enough. But there was a tightness, a containment, a strongly held sense of self that Cole felt when he moved through their world as one of them.

That sense dropped away. Any of the tension that had survived the drive, slid away as Cole walked deeper into the forest. His strides lengthened; his movements became fluid and his body loose in a way that wasn't exactly human. His nose filled with the scents of sun-warmed pine and the rich loam of the forest floor, and his skin tingled with sudden awareness. Here the air was heavy and lush, thick with myriad growing things—the sweetness of lavender and hyssop, the busy drone of harvesting bees, and the cool, earthy scent of mushrooms that flourished in the shadows.

With none of his superhuman senses closed off or ignored, Cole became as much a part of the woods as the trees or the squirrel that chittered above him. The extension of his senses and the feedback of the answering wilderness blurred the boundary between him and nature until one seemed no truer than the other.

He walked for an hour, until he could no longer sense the slightest trace of humanity. He stopped under a large tree. He took off his backpack. High up the mountain now, and still in the shade, the air was slightly cool. It was a relief to pull off his T-shirt, which was damp with sweat down the back and under his arms. His shoes followed, then his shorts, his underwear, until he stood naked. Cole tucked his clothes into his backpack and took a long drink from the two-liter water bottle he'd brought.

There was food in the backpack as well: two protein bars and a giant bag of the trail mix Jamie had made for the last time they'd all gone out together. Cole returned the water to the pack and zipped it closed. He swung one of the straps over his shoulder and jumped to grab one of the tree's lower limbs. He pulled himself up easily and swung to grab a second, higher limb. He slid the straps of the backpack over a branch and dropped to the ground.

Though it smelled enough of predator that his pack would probably have been safe enough from scavenging animals on the ground, Cole didn't want to end his run with a standoff against a bear. He'd win, probably, but had no real desire to find out. Or to ruin a bear's day because he'd been lazy.

Cole rolled his shoulders back, took a deep breath of the gloriously sea-scented forest air, and shifted.

He'd begun panting before he changed. The heat intensified now that his entire body was covered in a thick coat of fur. *Not the best planning*, he admitted with a wry, tongue-lolling grin. He should have waited until evening or planned ahead and gone early. No matter. He'd take a different route than he'd intended; he'd angle toward the stream and follow it.

He took off: burst of speed, paws digging eagerly into the loam and muscles thrumming with energy, body lower to the ground, elongated spine with tail for balance. Sensory input came in differently. He was more body, less mind. He moved with instinct and freedom; reactions were first and thought came second in a different mindset to move through a different world.

Knowing that overheating when he'd barely begun would be miserable, Cole slowed to a lope. He could detect the freshwater scent of the stream now, lighter under the briny scent of the ocean and the sharp pine of the trees, and followed it.

Everything that wasn't him, the woods, the air, or the water spilled away. His focus narrowed to the world immediately around him and expanded within that space. He stopped being Cole and started simply to be.

By the time he reached the stream he was hot enough that he'd slowed to a walk. He strode directly into the water. He dipped his head to drink and, once he'd satisfied his thirst, he lowered his body to rest as the cold water eddied around him.

Cooler now, he rose with water pouring from his pelt in streams. He shook and sent it flying—and wished suddenly, wrenchingly, that Nathan were there to yelp and scramble out of the spray. Angry with himself for letting that thought intrude, Cole picked his way out of the stream and took off on another run, leaving the image of a wet and affronted Nathan behind.

He stuck close to the stream, followed it to where it poured down a sudden drop into the woods. Cole came to a stop at the edge and sat, panting heavily.

The lake glimmered blue, framed by the gentle green hills that were almost mountainous. The cloudless sky was endless. It was easy here, easy to be a part of this ecosystem.

Part of him, always, wished quite simply to stay. It was not wanting, exactly, but an ache. It would be easy to exist like this. Others did, he was sure: lone wolves, as Ryn had been, possibly even entire packs.

Cole knew he couldn't live that way. It wasn't in him. A werewolf identity was difficult to describe. It wasn't as simple as movies and romance novels would have humans believe. There wasn't the wolf part and the human part of him—they weren't separate entities, each warring for control. He wasn't a wolf *or* a human. He was a werewolf: constantly, always, both. It was an identity of its own. No matter the physical form his body currently inhabited, he was never more of one and less of the other. And that meant that he needed his humanity as much as he needed this.

Cole lowered to his stomach and rested his head on his paws to doze in the heat.

HE AWOKE, HIS MOUTH FLOODED with saliva. The scent of prey filled his senses. He rose instantly.

Upwind was a young mule deer. Excitement wiped away the drowsiness of sleep, and he was moving.

Cole followed the scent; large paws were soundless as he padded closer. His entire body was on alert. Every rustle of leaves, snap of a twig, call of a bird registered. The deer was male, tined and cocky. As Cole neared, he could see each twitch of the deer's giant ears and his lips skinned back from his teeth.

The deer froze, and Cole stilled. It turned its head, and Cole crouched lower. The deer stared for a heartbeat, two, and then resumed its journey.

Cole followed, a silent and deadly shadow.

He didn't know for how many hours he stalked the deer. It caught his scent once and bolted. Cole gave it a moment's head start, then gave chase; his entire body was alight and electric as he raced after the deer.

In the end, he left it unharmed. He'd had no intention of taking it down, not really. Though he could eat an entire deer on his own, the resulting fullness and the nap he'd require seemed too much of a hassle. A deer brought down by and shared with pack was a different animal entirely.

He left the deer grazing unconcerned, convinced that it had outrun the predator, and headed back to where he'd left his bag. By the time he returned to his car, the parking lot had emptied significantly. The sun was setting; the light had gone rich and gold where it filtered through the trees.

Cole's body, human once again, thrummed pleasantly with the bone-deep contentment of a day spent unrestricted, of movements and mannerisms free of scrutiny.

He settled into the driver's seat and pulled out of the lot. As he followed the dirt road out of the woods winding toward the highway that would take him back to Vancouver, his wild awareness folded itself down. He no longer felt so acutely the intimate connection with the woods and the creatures in it. That part of himself would never be gone, but it could be quiet—a necessity for living in the city, for passing as a regular human.

As he pulled onto the highway, he flipped the visor down, cutting the glare of the sun as it sank toward the horizon. Halsey switched over to Tegan and Sara, and Cole's thumb tapped against the wheel to the beat.

He'd eaten the entire bag of trail mix on his way back to the car and remained ravenous. Maybe he'd stop by the grocery store on his way home and pick up a couple steaks to grill. He'd share with Kiara if she was home, and if not—two steaks weren't an entire deer, blood still hot as he sank his teeth into its soft belly, but would be a decent enough trade-off. And, he grinned, amused at the thought, maybe he'd grill them the bloody side of rare.

Cole took his eyes off the road and glanced at the clock on the dashboard. He should have just enough time to get to the store before it closed.

He took the bend in the road unthinking; his eyes drifted back just in time to see the crumpled body splayed across both lanes. Cole yanked on the wheel and jerked the car close enough to the edge that for a moment he was certain he would career down the mountain side. The car wasn't quite up to his superhuman reflexes and, as the acrid scent of burning rubber hit Cole's nose, all he could hope was that the car would *stop*.

It did, with a bone-jarring lurch, but safely off the road. Cole was up and out of his seat a split second later and beside the body in an instant. It wasn't human. Relief ran through him like water. He'd been fairly certain it wasn't, but it felt better to have that confirmed.

Cole crouched over the deer. Bloody and broken, its chest still rose and fell weakly. Brown eyes clouded with agony. Under the overpowering scents of panic, pain, and the violent crush of metal, a familiar one had Cole's invisible hackles rising.

It was his deer, the one he'd stalked late into the afternoon, the one he'd never intended to kill.

A bitter taste in his mouth, Cole placed his broad hand on the deer's furred side. There would be no recovery. The injuries were mortal; blood frothed at the deer's lips.

With a movement both merciful and brutal, he snapped the animal's neck and felt the body go limp beneath his hands.

Grief bowed his head.

Cole rose and hefted the body. It would have been a struggle—if not impossible—for a regular human, but to him the weight was nothing. He took the deer's body into the woods, far enough in that the inevitable scavengers would be safe from the deadly rush of vehicles.

Reluctant to simply stride back through the woods and to his car, he lingered over the body. Whatever connection he'd felt with the deer was one-sided. There was no reason for the hollowness in his stomach or the sorrow that slid like an eclipse over the pleasure of the day.

The deer's eyes stared, blank and sightless. Cole exhaled slowly and turned back to the car.

Chapter Seventeen |

Nathan forced his eyes open wider. If he could just *see* more, he'd keep his focus. The screen blurred; the grid, the black text seemed to swim under water. He was entering the data from his journals into a spreadsheet he'd created, hoping to group similar information.

However, his notes had become less professional and more confessional. Now, he couldn't skim the pages—he might miss a detail about his day that now had more meaning—so he had to read each entry carefully. It didn't help that Nathan was more of a Word guy than an Excel guy and found anything more than basic input wildly frustrating.

But once finished, he'd have an easier time connecting the dots. In TV and movies, the research-y guys—Nathan was irritatingly aware of the trope he fulfilled in his own personal werewolf story—always created dramatic research boards on their walls or a convenient expanse of glass. Multi-colored string was often involved, which Nathan had never been able to follow, and an apparently never-ending supply of thumbtacks. Since Nathan had none of those things—except his wall, but he wasn't losing his damage deposit—Nathan went with an ordinary, civilian, Excel spreadsheet.

And, on his third re-read of his journals, Nathan was almost finished. He'd gathered every detail he knew about the werewolves, every inhuman ability; every tell: eyes that changed color, vocal cords that produced sounds no human could manage, strength, speed, enhanced senses. Then, everything he knew about GNAAW—how the organization was structured, the number of registered packs, their corresponding locations, how they communicated. He entered the dates of each meeting Kiara's pack had had with the organization and listed response times to the various crises they'd faced. Then he'd pulled together all the information he had on the Huntsmen, including what little he'd gleaned from them during their time together in February, not just information about the Huntsmen themselves, but what *that* organization knew about werewolves.

He'd closed his blinds once the sun had begun to rise and had gone to full-screen on his desktop Mac. He had no idea what time it was. He didn't feel tired. Just... scratchy, a vague, itchy discomfort all over. A few hours ago—probably—he'd had to rummage in his medicine cabinet to find eye drops, left over from when he'd last decided he was through with glasses and wanted to return to contacts.

There was probably an expiration date on the eye drops, but Nathan was ignoring that. He was ignoring everything he could. Cole had texted. Nathan had left the phone upstairs then, remembering to reply only when his stomach had protested loudly that he needed to find something to eat.

He hadn't checked his phone since. He would when he was finished.

He was confident that tomorrow—or later tonight, or whatever time it was. *Later*—he'd be able to tease something out from his data. He knew more about the Huntsmen than anyone thought, not that he was hiding what he knew. It wasn't as if he'd been keeping things from the pack, from Dee. But what he knew came from the hours he'd spent with the Huntsmen, and Nathan didn't like to talk about it.

You know who we'll go to next, don't you? His shoulder jerked as the Huntress' phantom voice whispered in his ear. *If you don't help us, we'll go to her.*

He shook off the memory and, though the greasy-slick guilt remained, went to the next page in his journal. He was almost through; only a few pages were left. He wanted to keep working, to dig through the information he'd deemed important until he'd found what he was looking for, but he knew that his ability to focus was rapidly dwindling. The point of diminishing returns was just on the horizon—if he hadn't already passed it.

He read the final pages slowly, mouthing them word-by-word to make sure he didn't skip over anything. Once he was satisfied he had it all, Nathan hit *save* on his spreadsheet and closed the program.

He rose wearily from the chair and was surprised to find himself swaying unsteadily. It was definitely time to sleep. He grabbed a glass of water from the kitchen and took it up the stairs to his bedroom.

After he settled into bed, Nathan picked up his phone, figuring he'd shoot off a quick response to Cole or Dee, who probably both wondered why they hadn't heard from him all day. There were over a dozen notifications on the screen: Facebook, Instagram, Twitter updates, a text from Cole, three from Dee, one from Cris. Nathan stared at the screen; his thumb hesitated above it. The effort it would take to unlock his phone, read the messages from Cole and Dee, and craft a response that wouldn't result in either of them hounding him for more information seemed insurmountable. It was too much, right now, too much for today.

He plugged the phone into the charger on his bedside table and flicked off the lamp.

With the blinds still drawn over the windows downstairs, the loft was cast into a false twilight, not dark enough to be mistaken for night, but not the blinding brightness of the summer afternoon. Nathan pulled the covers up tight to his neck and burrowed his head into his softest pillow.

His body still felt strung-tight. The weariness of the last few hours was not quite enough to combat the frenzy of his thoughts that had kept him up this long. He closed his eyes and slowed his breathing. He would sleep. He had to believe that.

It seemed that was all he had these days: belief without proof. *Well, so be it.* He'd find the proof. Even if it killed him.

Kill or cure, the Huntress crooned. *One or the other. No middle ground.*

Nathan grabbed his other pillow and pressed it against the side of his head, hoping to drown out her voice as easily as he could drown out the noise of a neighbor's party.

Chapter Eighteen |

NATHAN PROPPED HIS CHEEK ON his chin as he stared dreamily at his office computer. Outside, cold February rain pelted at his window. The database he was attempting to reorganize was a jumble of colors and text on the screen, meaningless shapes as his mind returned, again and again, to the kiss he and Cole had shared last night in Nathan's loft.

They'd been creeping toward that irrevocable first kiss. The lines between them had blurred for months—a casual glance that lingered too long, the warm press of thigh against thigh as they sat closer than strictly necessary. Whatever it was that had held them both back had been wrecked the moment Cole had crawled into bed beside Nathan on the night the Huntsmen had found Dee and her wolves at the drag king show. Waking up with Cole's strong arms wrapped firmly around him and Cole's leg entwined between his, Nathan knew he was lost.

He'd held off—they'd both managed, whether that had been Cole taking his cue from Nathan or because Cole had been equally cautious about the growing connection between them—for another night. But Nathan, at least, was only human.

And he wasn't sure if it was a werewolf thing—he'd never kissed another werewolf—or a Cole thing, but the second Cole's lips had slid against his as they'd stood, the floor had opened beneath Nathan and he'd tumbled down, heart first.

In his sleep, Nathan's lips curved up in a smile, and he snuggled deeper into his bed as he sank deeper into the dream.

Chapter Nineteen |

NATHAN CHECKED HIS WATCH; IT was later than he'd realized. It got dark so early in February that it was easy to lose track of the time.

A knock sounded on his closed office door.

Nathan moved restlessly underneath his covers. "Come in," he called in his dream, anticipating Cris.

A woman stepped through the door. Nathan smiled, polite but puzzled. He didn't recognize her, though there was something about the spill of long, dark-red hair over her olive-colored coat that pinged in the back of his mind.

"Sorry, can I help you?"

"I think you can, Mr. Roberts. Will you?"

Nathan frowned, unease growing as he struggled to figure out what about the woman put him on edge.

She took another step into the room, and two large men filled the doorway behind her. They wore all black, mercenary-style clothing that looked as though they'd stepped right out of a *Call of Duty* game.

He had a confused moment of blankness, and then: *Huntsmen.*

Nathan jerked to his feet. His chair toppled behind him with a crash. He had no plan, no strategy. The Huntress—for surely, this was her—continued forward, and the two men followed her.

Nathan's thoughts tripped over each other. *What were the Huntsmen doing here?* If they'd found him here, found his work, they'd found his apartment as well. Wouldn't that have been their first stop? And, if it had been, what did it mean that the Huntsmen were here?

They must not have found what they were looking for. The realization blazed like heat through his veins: Kiara had gotten Ryn out, and the two wolves were still safe.

Nathan stared defiantly at the Huntress; his hands were curled into fists at his side. He said nothing. He would say nothing. He would give them nothing.

She held his look for a long, measuring moment, and then gave the man to her right a nod. The heavy-set bald man grinned and came around Nathan's desk.

Nathan gritted his teeth and fought. He lashed out with his fists, his feet; his struggle was silent and furious. His breath came in short, sharp pants. He managed to land a punch on the guy's ear, and the Huntsman swore. He grabbed a fistful of Nathan's shirt, pulled the collar choking-tight around Nathan's neck, and decked him.

Pain exploded across the side of Nathan's face. His vision blacked out, and in the handful of seconds it took to force his shocked body back into motion, the Huntsman slammed him against his office wall and held him there with a meaty hand at his throat.

Nathan's vision returned, but remained blurry. He'd lost his glasses. He tasted blood. The left side of his face was agony, and his ears rang. The hand at his throat tightened. Nathan grabbed the Huntsman's wrist and fought to tear it away as his airway narrowed.

A third man stepped into his office. He ignored Nathan and the other two Huntsmen, and addressed the woman, who watched Nathan's struggles impassively.

"This floor is clear, Ms. Vaughan."

"Thank you, Sandeep." The Huntress glanced around Nathan's office. "This space is too small. Is there another that will work?"

"A conference room at the end of the hall."

"Good. Bring him," she ordered, and followed the third man out of the room.

Nathan sucked in a huge, gasping breath as the first Huntsman removed his hand from Nathan's throat. He was given no time to recover; his arms were twisted behind his back until the strain on his shoulders was sharp enough to cut through the throbbing of his cheek.

"Hang on a sec." The second man, lanky and blond, retrieved something from the floor. "Wouldn't want to forget these," he said in a Southern drawl. He held the item up, and Nathan was able to make out the shape of his glasses. The man came forward and began to put them back on Nathan's face, but paused mid-way with a frown. "Oops. Guess they got a little busted."

The glass of one lens was shattered. The Huntsman holding Nathan laughed when his buddy shrugged and hooked the glasses onto the collar of Nathan's shirt. "I'd say we'll try and be more careful next time, but…"

"Lycan-lovers get what they deserve." The man behind Nathan finished. His voice was low and threatening in Nathan's ear as he wrestled Nathan out of his office.

"What does wolf pussy taste like, anyway?" He forced Nathan down the hallway. "Me and the guys have always wondered. And you seem to have quite the smorgasbord at your disposal."

Nathan's curled his lips back to display his bloody teeth and said nothing. As they approached the conference room, he could see the blurred shapes of Sandeep and the Huntress inside. Whatever they'd done to him already would only get worse. Nathan redoubled his struggles and tried to drop to the floor to make it more difficult for them to get him inside. The guy holding him just yanked on Nathan's twisted arms—the pain was vicious and lancing—until Nathan thought something might break. He got his feet back under him and stumbled forward.

Chapter Twenty

In his bed, Nathan moaned, low and pained. He didn't want to go into the room. He knew what would happen next. He turned, twisted himself farther into his sheets. *No, no, no, no*, he begged his dream-self.

"Thank you," the Huntress said, once the blond guy closed the conference room door behind them. "You can let him go, Allan," she told the bald man holding Nathan.

He released Nathan's arms, and Nathan winced as feeling returned to his hands. His overstretched shoulders ached.

"Mr. Roberts, I apologize for the inconvenience. We only need a few minutes of your time, and then you'll be free to go." She held up his phone, which she must have picked up from his desk during the struggle. "We need you to call your friend Kiara."

Nathan said nothing but stood angry and mute. Silence was his best and only defense.

Allan took a threatening step closer, and Nathan held up his chin, firming his jaw. They could hit him again. No way in hell would he make that call.

The Huntress waved off Allan. "I understand your reluctance, Mr. Roberts. This isn't about your friends, though, about the pack wolves.

We aren't here for them. This is about the other one. I promise you, we aren't going to hurt anyone else."

But they were going to hurt Ryn. A person didn't need a master's degree in library science to read between those lines.

"Look, we understand that you are just trying to keep your people safe. That's exactly what we are doing as well. We keep humanity safe. That's our goal here. We're human, just like you," the Huntress cajoled. "The pack wolves—they govern themselves. They keep themselves hidden; they follow the rules. They aren't trouble. It's the lycans who don't have a pack that cause trouble. Lone wolves are significantly more likely to hurt innocent, defenseless people. We only want to prevent that."

Nathan didn't care if the Huntress herself personally saved helpless babies from the slavering jaws of a rabid werewolf. There was nothing they could do to him that would make him cooperate. If they were going to hurt him more… well. Allan didn't seem to have a handle on his emotions. Nathan would rile him up until he hit too hard. He couldn't call Kiara if he was unconscious.

The Huntress responded to his continued silence with a regretful smile. "You know who we'll go to next, don't you?" she asked gently. "If you don't help us, we'll go to her. To Deanna. What's her address, again?" she asked Sandeep.

It was Allan who rattled it off, though.

White-hot and blinding, fury burned through Nathan. *Why did everyone have Dee's address? First crywolf and now these guys. Why was it so fucking easy to find?* He was going to have a word with the government, with the Internet, with the goddamn yellow pages. He was going to shove her and her girlfriend and her dog into witness protection on some godforsaken, off-the-grid farm in Saskatchewan. He would scrub every trace of her from every search engine known to man. He'd—

Allan grinned, and his teeth were sharp. His eyes were orange.

Fear replaced fury like a bucket of ice down his back. Nathan took a shallow breath.

"Fine," he bit out. "Give me my phone."

When he hung up, Nathan felt hot and dizzy all over. He handed the phone back to the Huntress and, ignoring the rest of the Huntsmen, pulled out a chair from the conference table and sat down. Careful of his still-throbbing cheek, he dropped his head into his hands, and prayed that Kiara had understood him.

The Huntress stepped out of the conference room with Sandeep behind her. After a handful of minutes, the three remaining Huntsmen took on more relaxed poses, one of them even going so far as to help himself to a bottle of water from the minifridge.

"What I don't get is why we didn't just take his phone and send a text? Why be so exposed, when all we needed was to swipe a kid's phone?" The third Huntsman muttered.

"That'd be 'cause," the blond man replied patronizingly, "with a text they know we have his phone. With a call they know we have *him*."

Nathan's head whipped up in horror as he realized the Huntress hadn't cared if Kiara had understood his warning. *He* was the bait—not the trumped-up text.

The two men turned to look at him, and their heads were no longer human, but black and furred, with fangs and glowing, orange eyes.

Nathan stumbled out of a chair for the second time that night. His arms pinwheeled as he dove out of the way when the third Huntsman—now Hunt*wolf*—moved toward him. The boardroom's glass windows shattered, and Nathan tumbled out.

He was yelling. He was yelling and fighting and the breath had been knocked out of him and his arms were trapped in the sheets and he couldn't—

In the sheets. In the sheets. Nathan's frantic breathing began to slow. He ceased his struggles and lay panting on the carpeted floor of his bedroom.

His heart still pounded wildly in his chest, and, though he was still, his body was tight with tension. It had been a nightmare—just another nightmare. The Huntsmen hadn't become crywolf-hybrids, and Kiara and the others had been smart enough to get out of the Huntress' trap.

"Fuck." He dropped his head back against the carpet.

How much sleep had he gotten? The dream—the nightmare—had felt like hours. If he'd gotten that much sleep, maybe the dream was worth it.

After a minute's solid struggle, Nathan finally tore out of his sheets. Legs wobbly, he eased himself up beside the bed and crawled slowly across the mattress. Without his glasses he had to squint to see the time on his phone. It was just past eight-thirty p.m. He'd only been asleep for a few hours, not as much as he'd hoped. Nathan dropped his phone on the bedside table. He should fix his sheets and lie back down. He couldn't, though. His skin felt as if it was covered in hundreds, thousands, of skittering ants.

He had to write down what he'd dreamt. It had come from memory, most of it. His subconscious had offered up that awful night like a demented gift. He'd lived though that night again as if it had been yesterday. Maybe there was something, something he'd missed the first time, something that would point him in the right direction.

Nathan grabbed his glasses and lurched out of bed.

Chapter Twenty-One |

COLE ARRIVED UNANNOUNCED AT NATHAN'S apartment Sunday morning. He hadn't heard from Nathan, not since that one blunt "can't" sent late Friday night. Cole left it for as long as he could—he respected Nathan's privacy, his agency—but, dammit, enough was enough. If Nathan wanted to hiss about his personal space and his freedom, he was more than welcome. Cole could take it. What he couldn't take was being iced out. If they were going to continue to be in a relationship—and it made him sick to consider the alternative—Cole needed to know that he'd be treated with basic decency and respect. If Nathan wasn't into that, if having Cole so close was causing him distress, Cole would step back.

He'd hate it, but he'd do it. If it meant Nathan had the space he needed to grieve, to heal, then Cole would return to simply being his friend. It was his last resort, but if Nathan wouldn't let Cole help and pushed him back every time, Cole wasn't sure what else he was supposed to do.

Cole shifted the donut box and the tray of coffee to his other hand, balancing the donuts on top of the coffee with an ease that would make a lifelong server jealous, then fit his key into Nathan's lock.

The door opened a few inches and stopped. Cole paused. He hadn't considered the swing lock. On one hand, he was glad Nathan was protecting himself. On the other hand, Cole's smooth breakfast-in-bed move was ruined.

He could leave. Cole clenched his jaw. He could turn around and go home. Kiara and Ryn would be glad of the donuts. Nathan would never have to know that he'd been here. He could wait and give it another day, at least.

No. He dropped his forehead against the barely open door and let out a heavy sigh. Waiting longer wouldn't make it easier, and it could very well make it uglier. A clean break was always easier to heal.

He swapped his keys for his phone and called Nathan. There was a fifty-fifty chance that Nathan had the phone on *silent*, and if so, Cole resigned himself to snapping the lock. He'd buy Nathan another lock and install it himself.

The phone rang, and Cole held his breath until the answering vibration sounded from inside Nathan's apartment. It rang once, then twice more before Nathan answered with a groggy "Whazzit?"

"I'm at your door. I brought donuts."

On the other end, the bedsheets rustled as Nathan sat up. Cole closed his eyes and braced.

"Cool."

"Cool?"

"Yeah, just—gimme a sec."

Cole's mouth dropped open and he closed it hastily. This was not the response he'd expected.

It took Nathan a minute to get out of bed and down the stairs. Cole waited while he unhooked the lock and swung open the door.

"Coffee too? You're a dreamboat." Nathan plucked one of the to-go cups from the tray and stepped aside to let Cole in.

"Uh, yeah." Cole followed Nathan to the couch; he was tense as he waited for the other shoe to drop. "Sorry for just showing up." *But I wasn't sure you'd answer my text.*

Nathan waved a dismissive hand and fished out a donut. "Mmph, no, this is good," he said around a mouthful of chocolate dip as he sat down.

Was it? Cole was thrown by Nathan's reaction. Nathan sounded more than happy to see him—a marked difference from "can't" followed by silence. Relief, guilt, and shame warred within Cole. Had he completely overreacted?

"Is everything okay? I don't mean to pry, but you dropped off for a bit there."

"I know." Nathan rolled his eyes and took a swig of coffee.

"You sleep?"

"Some." Nathan reached for a second donut. "I pulled one of Dee's Aunt Leita's special brownies from the freezer and got bonkers high. Played video games till I passed out. Sorry for the radio silence. I just didn't want to have to think for a bit, you know?"

"Yeah." Cole squeezed Nathan's knee, thinking of his solo run yesterday. "It looks like it did you good." He meant that too. The quiet air of despair that had followed Nathan around since he'd discovered his neighbor's body seemed to have vanished, along with the frustration he'd carried with it.

Fuck. Cole fought the urge to drop his head in his hands and settled for staring at his lap. He'd gone to DEFCON 1 when all Nathan had needed was a pot brownie and a night of video games. Cole's full-blown panic seemed wildly irrational in the face of Nathan's more settled demeanor. Whatever the days of silence had been, Nathan had clearly turned a corner.

Cole swallowed his guilt—he'd deal with that later—and cupped the back of Nathan's head in his hand. Nathan turned, blue eyes soft behind his glasses, and smiled as Cole bent to kiss him.

Nathan's lips parted gently under his. He tasted like chocolate, rich and dark. Peace settled through Cole when he finally pulled back; his body felt loose and warm with reassurance. This was solid; they were solid. Whatever was going on around them, they'd be able to return here, to this reverent press of lips against lips.

"I'm glad to see you. I'm sorry I didn't text first." Cole had jumped to ridiculous conclusions and regretted springing an unannounced visit on Nathan, though the relief at knowing things might be getting back to normal made it almost worth it.

"I'm glad to see you too."

"Do you have any plans for the day?"

Nathan gave him an amused sidelong look. He settled back into the couch. "I was thinking about watching some Netflix. Wanna join?"

"Yeah." Cole grinned. "That'd be nice."

Chapter Twenty-Two |

NATHAN HAD FORCED HIMSELF TO leave his phone upstairs the entire time Cole was over. If he had it in front of him, he'd be checking it nonstop. Besides, he'd done all he could last night when he'd reached out. He'd hear back—and he was certain he would hear back—but until then, he could do some damage control on his relationship with his boyfriend.

Cole's concern was something Nathan needed to shake off. He couldn't do what he intended to do with a worried Cole breathing down his neck. Nathan didn't feel good about lying—*weed and video games?* While that sounded like a great way to spend the weekend, Nathan had more important things to do. One was make sure he and Cole were good. Such an outright lie involved a certain meanness, but Cole disbelieved Nathan's premise that other supernatural beings existed, so what was the point in having a conversation that would only turn into a fight?

He'd apologize later, when he had his proof. And he'd deal with the guilt. It was worth it to patch over the breaking points between him and Cole. He'd tell all manner of lies if he must lie to keep them together—not *bad* lies, but white ones.

Nathan had a whole new perspective on the Willow-spelling-Tara *Buffy* storyline. But he wasn't going to go darkside, and Cole wasn't going to die. A musical episode would be cool, though.

Nathan brought his focus back to the TV and snuggled closer beside Cole. The episode of *The OA* was nearly over, and, since they both had to work tomorrow, he suspected this would be their last one.

Sure enough, as the credits rolled Cole tightened his arm around Nathan and dropped a kiss to the top of his head. "I should head home."

"Mmm." Nathan tucked his head into the bend of Cole's neck. "Let's have impromptu-donut-and-TV-show-marathon Sundays more often."

"Agreed." Cole rose. "Are you going to be okay tonight? I just mean—I can stay, if you want. If that'll help you sleep."

Nathan was tempted. The thought of crawling into bed beside Cole, laying himself down against the solid bulk of him, closing his eyes, and knowing without a doubt that he was utterly safe was almost more appealing than he could bear.

He wouldn't be able to check if he'd heard back from the Huntsmen though. He'd somehow managed to lie this morning; Cole had been too stiff to pay attention to Nathan's heartbeat. If Cole had caught him in the lie, Nathan wasn't sure what he would have done—probably blamed it on insomnia and crossed his fingers. Nathan hadn't felt weird about the werewolves being able to tell when he was lying until he had something to lie about. And he wasn't going to push his luck by lying twice in one day.

"No, I think I'll be good. Thanks though. I appreciate the offer." If Nathan figured out what kind of thing Jag had been, though, what else was out there, maybe his brain would stop being all twisted up and his nightmares would stop. Then Cole could stay the night because he *wanted* to, not because he was worried about Nathan. Knowing the person in your bed was there out of concern and pity, not for their desire or comfort, was shitty, even if it did, admittedly, help him sleep.

Whatever. He was getting closer now. It wouldn't be much longer until everything went back to normal.

Cole gathered his things, and Nathan walked him to the door. He pulled Nathan in for a long hug. "Today was really nice. Thank you."

"Yeah." Nathan pulled back, a little startled at the emotion in Cole's voice. *Had things gotten that tricky between them that a day spent watching TV was noteworthy?*

He ignored his guilt. He'd get them back on track. He would. He could have both Cole and his search for the truth.

"I'll see you soon, okay?" Nathan promised as he opened the door. Cole nodded and stole one more kiss on his way out.

Nathan waited, holding his breath, beside the closed door until he heard the elevator doors ding open and then close. He sprinted across the apartment and up the stairs, taking them two at a time, to his bedroom where he snatched his phone off the bed.

He had half a dozen responses to the Missed Connection ad he'd posted last night.

Huntress - M4W

Ms. Vaughan,

You like hunting and hate werewolf movies. We met in a library, where you and your friends left a mark. Wish I'd gotten your number—I hate to be cryptid, but I have something I think you'll be interested in.

He particularly liked the cryptid-cryptic wordplay. Most people would dismiss it as a typo, but she'd know.

Most of the responses were bullshit: bots and people who were lonely or bored.

Hi, I'm not the woman you're looking for, but…

Fan of werewolves? Join our Wolf's Run LARP pack…

He'd have to tell Deanna about that one, once he was able to tell Deanna about any of this.

Want to meet women? Game the system! Learn these nine simple steps to…

Fucking pick up artists. Nathan rolled his eyes, and the hope he'd felt began to falter. Maybe his clever ad hadn't been as clever as he'd thought. Nathan clicked on the last response.

I didn't expect to hear from you again, Mr. R. Looking forward to reconnecting.

The email was signed with a simple H.

He jumped off the bed and whooped in excitement. His nightmare about the Huntsmen had been crucial—what with everything that had happened the night they'd ambushed him in his office, he'd forgotten one small, crucial detail. Through the dream, his subconscious had taken pity on him.

He'd heard her name. And the post had worked.

Nathan shot off a response to her email; his fingers flew over the screen of his phone.

I have information you'll be interested in. Can we meet?

He paced his room while he waited. It didn't take long.

Is there a reason we can't do this over email?

Nathan scowled.

I need to talk to you. You owe me this.

He waited. Nathan chewed on his lower lip and wondered if he hadn't pushed too far. If she refused to talk with him, he wasn't sure what—

His phone vibrated.

I don't owe you anything. However, I will be in Vancouver two days from now.

Nathan did an awkward butt-shaking victory dance. He could wait two days.

You know where I work. Let's grab coffee on campus.

He knew the reactions from Dee and the pack to his meeting with the Huntress would range from shock, to horror, to downright fury (Kiara). And while Nathan could understand that, he wasn't an idiot. He wasn't going to meet her anywhere private. They'd be in public and in broad daylight. Besides, he was human. And Ryn was pack now, so the wolves were safe.

Fine. I'll be in touch.

Chapter Twenty-Three

IN THE FEW HOURS BEFORE his meeting with the Huntress, Nathan was completely unable to focus on work. He sat at his desk; his leg bounced in a jittery rhythm as he stared mindlessly at the screen. He'd printed out everything he knew about Jag and about his death. He'd gone over it and over it again, until he finally tucked it into a folder and stuffed it his bag.

She'd know. She'd have to. Or have some idea, anyway. A direction to point him in. He'd know something at least.

Half of him was horrified at what he planned to do. The audacity of this betrayal wasn't like Nathan. The Huntsmen had *literally hunted* some of Nathan's best friends earlier this year. And those same Huntsmen had threatened Nathan and Dee with bodily harm. *These people weren't safe.*

And Nathan was risking bringing them back into the wolves' lives for, what? To prove a point?

No, he insisted to the parts of him that were still trying to talk himself out of it. *I'm uncovering a secret. I'm making sure we know what's out there so we can be safe. I'm protecting us.*

Either way, it was too late to back out now.

His phone chimed with the calendar reminder. His meeting was in fifteen minutes. Nathan took a deep breath and rose from his desk.

He grabbed his shoulder bag and took one last look around his office before he stepped out and closed the door behind him.

He texted Dee as he crossed the campus.

If you don't hear back from me in an hour, I'm at Great Dane Coffee.

She texted back within seconds. **?????**

Nathan switched his phone to silent and tucked it into the front pocket of his bag. He spotted the Huntress as he neared the cafe. She sat at one of the patio's small round tables and two iced coffees sat on the table in front of her. She'd kept her hair down, and it billowed an unnervingly dark reddish-brown in the warm summer breeze. At the table behind her, two muscular men, both decades too old to be university students, sat with studied nonchalance.

Despite the heat, Nathan felt a chill. He hefted his bag more firmly onto his shoulder and strode forward.

She watched him impassively as he sat across from her. Her eyes were unreadable behind her fashionable, gold-framed sunglasses.

"Well?" she asked, finally.

"Here." Nathan pushed the second iced coffee aside—as if he'd put anything in his mouth she'd touched—and laid his folder on the table.

The Huntress pursed her lips and slid the pages toward her. She lifted her drink and took an absentminded sip from her straw as she read. Nathan forced himself to lean back against the chair and attempt to appear relaxed.

When she finished, the Huntress raised her head and pushed the file back to Nathan. "What is this supposed to mean?" She gestured at the printouts, the copied pages of Nathan's recent journal entries about Jag. "I thought you said you had information for me."

"I do." Nathan leaned forward. "I want to know what he was."

"What do you mean, what he was?" The Huntress shook her head. "He was nothing. A victim. If you knew him, I'm sorry." She gave an eloquent shrug. "But I can't help you solve a murder."

"No." Nathan shook his head and pushed the printout of the news article in her direction. "Look at how he was killed." He jabbed his finger at the paper. "Look! That's your kind of thing. Taking the head, the hands? Tell me that's not how you'd kill a werewolf."

The words tasted like ash in his mouth. He didn't want that to be something that he'd thought of, that he'd put thought into, but it was. He'd witnessed first-hand the incredible healing powers of werewolves. If he wanted to kill one, he'd want to do it in a way he'd be sure would be permanent. Beheading was the logical step.

The Huntress leaned forward over the table and gestured for Nathan to come closer. Eyes narrowed with suspicion, he bent his head toward her.

"When I kill a werewolf," she said softly. "I don't leave a body for the police to find."

Nathan jerked back, disgust and anger written on his face. "That's it, then? That's all you have for me."

"*You* were supposed to have something for *me*," the Huntress reminded him pointedly. "What is it?"

"What is—" Nathan broke off, incredulous. "This. It's this!" He jabbed again at his research. "There can't just be—" He caught himself and lowered his voice. "There can't just be werewolves. There must be other stuff. Other shifters. Other creatures that we think are myth but are real. Vampires. Sorcerers. Fairies! This proves that there are things out there that are harder to kill than we are." *She had to understand, didn't she? Out of everyone, out of all the people who knew about werewolves, surely she'd see where he was coming from.*

She tilted her head. "You really think you're an expert now that you've learned what some of your friends are?"

Nathan's nostrils flared at the insult, but he bit his tongue.

"Werewolves aren't mythical creatures, Mr. Roberts. Werewolves are people. People who are afflicted with a disease. They have lycanthropy. It's a genetic disorder. It makes them dangerous; it doesn't make them fantastical. And it doesn't mean that... that gnomes are real." Her lips quirked; she was amused at her joke. "You've connected dots that aren't connected. And it's impressive work, I'll give you that, but you're stumbling around blind in the dark. Stop." She took a sip of her iced coffee and settled back into her chair.

"If you'd just take a *look*—" Nathan started.

"I have. It's murder. I'd lay money on the girlfriend or a coworker, someone who's watched one too many episodes of CSI and hoped getting rid of their victim's head and hands would be enough to hide the body's identity. Idiot."

She shuffled through his file. "This is good work, though. You know how to dig, how to do your research. We could always use more folks with your focus." She arched an eyebrow over the top of her sunglasses. "Any interest in coming to work for the other side? We pay better than your university, and you already know what it is we hunt."

"What? You want me to—what? No. No. Absolutely not." Nathan shook his head vehemently; his skin crawled. That she could even *think* he'd consider it was horrifying.

"Very well, then. I won't waste any more of my time." She stood and picked up her coffee. "Don't reach out to me again, Mr. Roberts."

"I won't," he said shortly. She sauntered away from the coffee shop. The two Huntsmen followed.

Nathan curled his hands into fists in his lap and forced himself to sit and not run after her. She'd given him nothing. And the worst part was, he didn't think she was lying. She was confident that werewolves—lycanthropes, to her—were the only aberration.

Defeated, Nathan sighed and gathered up his file. He stuffed it back into his bag and warily eyed the ice coffee. Moisture had beaded down the sides of the plastic cup, and the ice was beginning to melt. He pushed back from the table with a scowl and grabbed the coffee. He tossed it, untouched, into the closest garbage can and went into the café to get his own coffee.

Waiting in line, he checked his phone. He had about a million texts from Dee. Despite his frustration and the accompanying exhaustion, he grinned reading them.

Nathan

This is a very alarming text, I'm sure you know that

Nathan

Nathan what are you doing

NATHAN

You're so lucky I am not a werewolf or I would hunt you down right now myself.

You'd better hope I don't go get my werewolf and have her do just that.

I'm so mad at you right now.

NATHAN

God.

A gif of an anxious looking Annie from the TV show *Community*.

It's been 47 minutes you better get your ass back.

WORRIED NOW

I'm fine, he texted her a response. **Sorry. Coffee with this guy from a hookup app. You can't be too safe!**

Dee began typing almost the second after Nathan had hit send. The ellipses bubbled on his screen.

Why didn't you just say that? JFC. And since when did you start meeting for coffee first?

Trying to be more responsible.

How was the 'coffee'

Nathan thought back to his encounter. **Hot, but sketchy. Won't see him again.**

All right. Well, if he was sketchy I'm glad you texted. Don't do that again though! You scared me.

Like, text me again, but don't be mysterious about it

You know

Nathan rolled his eyes. **I know,** he sent as he stepped up to the counter.

"Hi, I'll have a large iced coffee, please. With an extra expresso shot." He hoped it would help him get through the rest of his workday.

Chapter Twenty-Four

NATHAN HAD HOPED TALKING WITH the Huntress would give him something—validation, at least, if not an outright answer. He replayed their conversation over and over, poking at it like an old bruise, even now, hours later.

He hopped off the crowded, sweltering bus a stop early and took the slight detour to the grocery store.

Maybe—and it sucked, deeply sucked, to be even thinking about admitting this, but—maybe she'd been right. Maybe Cole was right. Maybe everyone was right, and Nathan was wrong. Maybe it *was* just humans and werewolves.

Was that better or worse than having a neighbor brutally murdered in his apartment building for no apparent reason?

Grateful for the grocery store's air conditioning, Nathan picked up a basket and headed to the produce section. He rounded the corner and almost ran into someone. He stopped just short and apologized instantly.

"Sorry, too much in my own head." *Wasn't that the truth?* "Oh, hey—it's Emily, right?" He recognized the woman from his building.

"Right." She nodded. Her strawberry hair was pulled back into a ponytail, and she had a yoga mat rolled up under her arm. Nathan started to move past and continue his shopping, but she grabbed his wrist and he stopped, surprised.

"I wanted to say—I mean, I'm sorry. For screaming. For telling the cops that you—that you—" Her voice hitched; her hazel eyes swelled with tears. "I'm sorry I told them you hurt Jag. They said you didn't, that you'd just found him first. They said that you were trying to help him. So, I'm sorry that I screamed." A tear rolled down her cheek, and she hastily wiped it away.

"It's okay." Guilt weighed like a stone in his stomach. He'd been so wrapped up in *what* Jag was, that he hadn't considered *who* Jag was. "I'm sure I would have done the same thing, if I saw what you'd seen. Did you, uh, did you know him?"

"Yes." Another tear trailed down her cheek. "We were friends. We were supposed to go see *Hamilton* together. Now I've got an extra ticket, but I don't want to take anyone but him." She looked at him; her eyes pled for some sort of answer.

Shit. "I'm sorry, Emily. That's really—that sucks," Nathan finished weakly.

"I hope they find out who did it. I hope they find out soon." Emily's voice went fierce; anger darkened her face. "He was a good person and he didn't deserve that."

"He didn't." Nathan rubbed a hand awkwardly against the back of his neck. "I'm sorry," he said, again, for lack of anything better to say.

Dammit, maybe Jag was just a regular guy. Maybe this was all in Nathan's head. "Well, listen, I gotta finish up here, but... I'll see you around?"

Emily sniffed and nodded. "He was magic, you know," she said as Nathan started to walk away.

"What?" Nathan's head whipped back aground. "He was what?"

"Magic. You couldn't be sad or angry around him. He made you feel good just to be in the same room."

Nathan's mind raced. *A glamour? Some sort of witchcraft? Sorcery?* That would explain why Jag's killer had taken his hands. A person without hands couldn't cast a spell or brew a potion.

"Hey, who's this guy? He bugging you?" A broad-shouldered, obnoxiously handsome man came up behind Emily and laid a possessive hand around her waist as he glared at Nathan.

"No, no." Emily brushed away her tears. "Travis, this is Nathan. He lives in my building."

Travis continued to glower, apparently not reassured. "Dangerous building," is all he said.

"It's not, usually." Nathan didn't know why he thought it was important to defend the place where someone had recently been beheaded, but this guy looked like a tool.

Travis lifted his eyebrows before dismissing Nathan's presence. "Are you done, babe?" he asked Emily, shifting his stance as he asked and effectively blocking Emily from Nathan's view.

Nathan rolled his eyes behind Travis's stupidly muscular back. Toxic masculinity was never more evident than in gym-rat culture. He bent around Travis and lifted a hand to Emily. "See you around."

"Bye." She returned his wave with a smile that didn't quite reach her sad eyes.

Nathan mentally flipped off Travis and continued to the produce section. Wanting to get back to his place as soon as possible, he grabbed what he needed in a hurry.

IT WAS STILL UNCOMFORTABLY HOT when Nathan left the grocery store, not that he expected a dramatic change in the fifteen minutes he'd been inside, but the lack of windows and the recycled air always made Nathan feel as he'd stepped into a different world. Returning to the bright sun and heat of the summer afternoon was jarring.

Nathan lifted a hand to shade his eyes and squinted behind his glasses. He'd left his prescription sunglasses on his kitchen counter and resolved to put them in his bag as soon as he got home so he wouldn't make the same mistake tomorrow.

At least he'd remembered his reusable grocery bag, he comforted himself. He firmed his grip on it and took the short cut through the alley. *A mistake*, he realized, half a block in when the cloying stench of rotting garbage invaded every pore of his body. He gagged, more from reflex than a need to vomit. He breathed shallowly through his nose.

A crow screamed above him, and Nathan jumped. He looked up, one eye closed against the sun, when it screamed again. It lifted from its perch on a fire escape and flew to land on a garbage bin a few yards ahead of Nathan.

He eyed it warily as he walked past. The second he began to relax, it shrieked furiously and flew over him so low that he ducked; he felt the brush of air from its wings.

"Jesus," he muttered. His heart fluttered, much to his chagrin. *It was just a bird.* He'd seen actual *werewolves*.

The flutter in his chest sharpened to a stab of fear when the crow once again landed ahead of Nathan on another fire escape. Nathan took a deep breath and choked on the smell. He coughed, and the bird shrieked. He stopped and struggled to catch his breath as he watched the bird with watering eyes.

It fell silent and cocked its head. Nathan blinked away tears as the crow's black, beady eyes regarded him.

When he began to breathe more normally, Nathan straightened. The crow screamed, a sound so loud that Nathan's ears echoed with it after it stopped. No small stab now, fear twisted a cold knife inside him. *Was this normal? Did crows do this?*

He glanced behind him. If he went back and took the long way, it would take an extra fifteen minutes. The bag of groceries hung heavy in his hand; the fabric cut into his skin. No, sticking to the alley would have him home in five minutes. He was overreacting. He probably walked by the crow's nest or territory or whatever.

"All right, I'm sorry." Nathan raised his hands in a harmless gesture meant to placate. Whether or not it would work on a crow, he wasn't sure, but he was willing to try it. "I'm gonna go on my way now. Cool?"

It was evidently *not* cool. The crow watched as he walked past it, then flew, shrieking, over his head.

"Fuck!" Nathan swore and ducked with a hand over his head. He heard the thunder of his pulse in his ears and tasted copper.

He was magic. Emily's voice whispered in his head.

Familiars. Witches and sorcerers had familiars. Demons in the form of small animals or birds they bonded with, that helped them come in to their powers. What would happen to a familiar if its sorcerer died? If they were murdered?

Nathan's feet were leaden as he stumbled forward in a near run. The crow screamed nonstop now, an awful, ugly cry. Nathan's breath was ragged; the reek of the garbage was forgotten.

The crow flew once more over him, and Nathan broke into a dead run when he had to go past it. It didn't follow. It clung to the twisted-open lid of a garbage bin, and Nathan heard its screams all the way to his building.

He ducked into the mouth of the parkade and leaned forward with his hand splayed across the warm concrete. He panted. His shirt was damp with sweat, and the aftertaste of terror was thick on his tongue.

What the fuck.

Chapter Twenty-Five

NATHAN WASN'T SURE WHAT IT was about the month of July, but, more often than in any other month that year he was being strong-armed into dinners with his friends. He didn't resent it, because he liked his friends, but he was frustrated because it took time he'd rather spend unravelling the mystery of his dead neighbor.

He stood outside of Deanna's apartment, the new one, a floor above the tiny bachelor apartment she and Arthur had shared before she'd moved in with Jamie. He'd picked up the required bottle of pinot gris for Deanna and a growler of beer for himself. Nathan gave himself a quick shake, trying to literally shake off his irritation and impatience. Dee was one of his favorite people, he reminded himself. And, if he was being honest, he probably did need to take a night off.

Mollified, Nathan used his key and let himself in. Arthur set on him immediately; the golden retriever's full body wriggled as he pressed himself as close to Nathan as possible. Nathan laughed and bent to give Arthur a thorough rub.

"Who's a good boy?" Nathan cooed. Any residual resentment vanished as Arthur collapsed to the floor and displayed his belly for Nathan's rubbing pleasure. "You're a good boy, Arthur! You're the *best* boy!"

Arthur's tail thumped in wild abandon against the floor.

"He missed you." Dee came out of the kitchen. Her hair was up in a bun, and she wore an old T-shirt and a pair of baggy pajamas.

"I missed him." Nathan gave Arthur one last pat, straightened, and crossed the room to wrap Dee in his arms. "I missed you, too." He closed his eyes and inhaled the comforting rose scent of her favorite shampoo.

Dee returned his tight hug, though it smooshed her glasses up against his chest and her cheek. They broke apart laughing.

"It's good to see you. And don't tell the others." Dee dropped her voice even though they were alone in the apartment. "But I'm glad we get to have a night just us."

"Me too," Nathan agreed. He put the booze on the counter and found the appropriate glasses. He loved the pack, of course, as did Dee. But not too long ago, it had just been the two of them. And now it had been too long since it was just the two of them.

"Where's Jamie tonight?" Nathan asked as he poured.

Dee slid onto a bar stool. "She also has 'normal' Friday night plans. She's having drinks with a couple of her classmates."

"Look at us." Nathan passed Dee a glass of the white wine and held up his pint. They cheers-ed, and each took a drink.

"Thanks for bringing wine." Dee closed her eyes and hummed.

"Thanks for buying pizza."

Dee's eyes blinked open. "Pizza night it is," she acknowledged with a grin.

"Good," Nathan said. Depending on who hosted, they traded off the alcohol and takeout purchases. He stuck the bottles in the fridge and took his beer into the living room. Dee grabbed her wine and joined him.

They settled comfortably on each end of the couch, facing each other. Arthur gave a heroic lunge and hauled himself between them. He circled awkwardly, his tail nearly knocking Dee's glass from her hand, before he settled down on the teal cushions with a heavy "woof."

By the time they'd picked a Netflix movie and gotten the pizza, they'd had a chance to catch up on most of their major stuff. *Wolf's Run* had hired a new DevOps Engineer and she was letting Deanna become more involved in the programming aspects of the game. Nathan's work was sending him to a conference in Ottawa in the fall. Jamie had begun swimming before she came home from school, claiming that to take the 99 bus home at five p.m. was hell, and she'd much rather spend that hour at the pool. Dee felt as though every time she walked into the bathroom she was smacked in the face with a wet swimsuit. Cole continued to send gently probing check-in texts to Nathan, which made him feel like a patient, not a partner. Arthur had been cornered by an angry cat the other day and was still trying to recover. Jamie had rescued him—though the cat had taken a swipe at her.

"Hah," Nathan snorted. He could picture Jamie's stricken look as she jumped back, unwilling to harm the cat in any way and overly cautious of her werewolf strength.

"That was the maddest cat I've ever seen." Dee shook her head; she kept her eyes on the TV as she took another slice of their loaded veggie deluxe. "I thought it was going to follow us back home."

Nathan frowned, thinking of the furious crow that had nearly followed him home. "The cat—did Jamie sense anything weird about it? Did it smell like a cat, or sound like a cat? A normal cat?"

"Nathan…" Pity softened Dee's features. "I think you need to let this go."

"Let what go?" he snapped.

"You know what I mean."

"Do I?" Nathan grabbed the remote and paused *Diary of a Teenage Girl.*

Dee suppressed a sigh. "I know this has been a shitty year. I know processing this stuff—"

"By 'this stuff' you mean 'surprise! These mythical monsters are real!'?"

"Yes," she said impatiently. "I get it. Trust me. I do. And that's why you need to trust me when I say, trust Cole. Trust Kiara. I can't believe I have to even *ask* you to trust Jamie."

"I don't not trust them," Nathan argued. "I don't trust GNAAW. I don't trust that it's just werewolves. Doesn't that seem insane to you? That, with everything…" He gestured widely. "…the whole canon of mythical creatures and it's *just werewolves* that are real? How does that make sense?"

"I don't know! I'm not a scientist. I'm not a, a biologist or an anthropologist. But I trust that the people who'd be in a better position to know than us—the until-recently-secret werewolves—are the authorities on the matter!"

"Why? Why do you trust them?"

"Because…" Deanna threw up her hands in frustration. "Because who else am I supposed to trust? Who else is figuring it out?"

"Me, Dee." Nathan said, stung. "I am. Why do you believe them and not me?"

"Oh, Nathan." Deanna leaned across the couch and put her hand on his thigh. "I believe you. I believe that you've had a year more eventful than most peoples' entire lives. I believe that *you* believe it. But I don't know if I believe that it's true. I'm sorry." Her green eyes pleaded with him to understand.

"No, you believe because Jamie says that it's just werewolves."

"Nathan."

"Admit it. You believe her over me. If it was us, just you and me, and we discovered *werewolves* existed, don't you think we—independent of said werewolves—would wonder what else there was? If you didn't have one in your bed, can you tell me, honestly, that you wouldn't mistrust an entire freakin' different species whose whole safety net was built around the lie that they didn't exist?"

Dee withdrew her hand and leaned against her side of the couch. Between them, Arthur whined.

"But that isn't the case, and I trust Jamie," Deanna explained patiently. "If the wolves knew about other mythical creatures, or whatever, that were real, they would tell us. And since they haven't, I think it's safe to say that there aren't."

"*Jamie* would tell you."

"What's that supposed to mean?"

Nathan shrugged. "Maybe Jamie doesn't know."

"Seriously, Nathan?"

"Maybe she doesn't. She's not an Alpha."

Deanna raised her eyebrows. "All right, even supposing that was true—Jamie not being a high enough 'rank' or whatever to be in the know—Kiara is an Alpha now."

"Oh, come on." Nathan scoffed. "You really think she'd tell us? No." He shook his head. "She's pack first. And I'm not faulting her for that…" He held up a hand, preempting Dee's indignant response. "…but if she thought she had to keep the secret to ensure the safety of her pack? You'd better believe she'd lie to the humans."

"Fine." Deanna rolled her eyes. "Kiara wouldn't tell you. She'd tell Cole though, and Cole would tell you."

Nathan shook his head. "Not if Kiara told him not to. If his sister who also happened to be his Alpha said the knowledge had to be pack-only, he'd obey."

"I *am* pack." Deanna's eyes blazed and color flared high on her cheeks. "Don't do this."

"Do what?"

"Divide us. Us against them." She gestured at a photo on the wall: a young Jamie and her two cousins beamed out at them.

"It *is* us against them. Or, no," Nathan corrected. "I don't mean it like that. Not against them. But, Dee…" And now his voice gentled. "…you're not pack."

Deanna's head flew back, and she looked as shocked as if he'd slapped her. "Why would you say that?"

Nathan ran a frustrated hand through his hair. "Because it's true. Look, I don't want to hurt you—"

"Then you're doing a shitty job."

"—but I'm telling the truth. You *aren't* pack. Have you ever looked at that statue thing? That figurine…" Nathan wriggled his fingers to indicate the small metal sculpture of four wolves leaping over a stream that GNAAW had presented to Kiara when she officially became Alpha of the Vancouver pack. "…the names of the pack members are engraved on the base. And yours isn't one of them." Now Nathan, gaze earnestly locked onto Deanna's, leaned forward. "I've read their official GNAAW literature, the fucking welcome package, the FAQ's." The only thing he hadn't read was GNAAW's online content, and that was because he hadn't been able to find Kiara's log in information and he had yet to stoop so low as to rifle through her bedroom drawers. Things left out in plain sight, on the other hand, or tucked into the bookshelf in the living room…

"You need four adult werewolves to form a pack. Werewolves, Dee. Not humans. Yeah, they're cool with wolves shacking up with humans, but we don't count as pack. Not really. It will always be wolves first. And I'm not upset about it," he said earnestly. "I get it. They have to protect their own, and that's fair. But it does mean that there's an *us* and a *them*. So, do you really think Jamie will always be honest with you?"

Dee was silent. Her arms were crossed over her chest, and she wouldn't look Nathan in the eye. "I think," she said finally, "that you should go."

"What? Dee. C'mon." Nathan rolled his eyes. "Obviously Jamie cares about you, of course she does. I'm not saying that you aren't important, that she doesn't love you, I'm just saying—"

"Stop." Dee met his gaze. "I'm serious."

"So am I! Don't be naïve, Dee. There's clearly—"

"Nathan, I don't want to keep talking about this. And, frankly, I don't want to talk to you at all right now. So you need to go, before I say something I'll regret."

Nathan opened his mouth, but closed it again without protest. Fine. If she wanted him to go, he would. He got up, grabbed his bag off the floor, stopped to shove his shoes on, and then he was out. The heavy door swung closed behind him with a bang.

Chapter Twenty-Six

HE CLATTERED DOWN THE STAIRS and pushed through the building's doors with more force than necessary. He was pissed: with himself, with Dee. He shoved his hands in his pockets. Walking, it would take nearly forty-five minutes to get home, but with his temper boiling in his veins, Nathan didn't have the patience to wait for a bus or track down a carshare.

He couldn't believe she'd asked him to leave. *Talk about an overreaction.* Nathan had only been trying to get her to see things from his point of view. And he wasn't wrong! Dee wasn't pack. That wasn't Nathan making shit up to be a jerk, that was the GNAAW-awful truth.

Wolves were pack. It was simple. It certainly wasn't worth Dee getting so mad over. Nathan scowled, and kicked a fallen pinecone.

The air was muggy and weighted down with smoky haze. Forest fires were a concern every summer, and this year the ones in British Colombia had been especially bad. The smoke had drifted down from the interior and settled over Vancouver early that morning and was expected to linger for at least the next few days.

Nathan liked the shrouded sun and the woodsy, campfire scent. It suited his mood—blunt and destructive.

Fire, now there was another way Nathan would kill something supernatural. It was easier than beheading, and a lot less messy. He'd probably still remove the head, unless he somehow managed to reduce the body to ash, but once the corpse was charred there'd be no blood to worry about.

Okay, he really had to stop being so morbid, even in his own head. As he waited at an intersection for the light to change, Nathan took off his glasses and rubbed at the bridge of his nose. He'd stop being so morbid, he promised himself, once he was able to put this whole Jag thing to bed.

If *it ever got put to bed.* It had been weeks since he had found Jag's body, and he was no closer to confirming his suspicions. He thought about what he did know. *Whoever had killed Jag had taken his hands— that was deliberate. A person doesn't just accidentally cut off another person's hands. Not* both. *The head, the hands, plus the truly bizarre animal stuff…*

Nathan was pretty sure he was on the right track. Sorcery, real life sorcery, seemed wacko on paper, he could acknowledge that. *But so did werewolves!* And—excitement at his line of thinking put an extra spring in his step as he crossed the street—being a sorcerer would be a lot easier to hide than being a werewolf. If anything, the Huntsmen claiming to know nothing about sorcerers or magic or other paranormal shit was almost proof that it was real. Just as when he'd begun to hunt for information about werewolves and GNAAW in the texts and databases at the library, the very *lack* of any concrete information about werewolves and how they organized had been *telling.*

Now, he just had to figure out how to fill in the missing pieces. He wondered… *no. That was too crazy. That was crossing a line. But… what if there was something in Jag's apartment?*

Breaking and entering was a crime. Obviously.

Was it really *breaking and entering when it was another unit in his building? That was less breaking and more… visiting.* And it wasn't as though anyone would be home to catch Nathan in the act. Besides, it wasn't as though Nathan would take anything. He only wanted to look.

His phone rang, and Nathan jumped nearly a foot in the air. "Jesus," he muttered as his heart rate returned to normal. He expected Dee, calling to apologize and to tell him to come back, but Cole's face filled the screen. Nathan answered.

"Hey."

"Oh! Hey!" Cole's voice held a note of pleasant surprise. "I didn't actually expect you to answer. I figured you'd be busy with Dee and I'd just get your voicemail."

"Hah." Nathan's laugh was clipped and bitter.

Confused silence from Cole's end. "Did something happen with you two?"

"She kicked me out."

"What? Why?"

"I don't know what her deal is right now. It wasn't even about her—so I don't know why she got all worked up. It's not like I told her something she didn't already know."

"What happened, Nathan? What did you tell her?"

Nathan rolled his eyes to the hazy sky. He didn't want to explain himself to Cole, though it would be nice to have someone on his side. He and Dee hadn't had a major fight in years, and Nathan needed Cole to see that he was in the right. "That she's not pack. Not really."

"Yes, she is. You know you could be too, right?" Cole had never asked Nathan.

"No, she's not. And I wouldn't be either."

"What are you talking about?"

"I know, okay? I know that humans aren't *really* pack. Dee's name isn't alongside yours on that statue from GNAAW. I've gone through all the pack-related literature GNAAW left for Kiara." That was a lie. He'd gone through everything that GNAAW had left, not just the pack-specific stuff, but now wasn't the best time to mention that. He wanted Cole to be on his side, after all. "Wolves are the only pack that counts, that really counts. And it's not like she shouldn't have already known that." That was what irritated Nathan the most about the argument. *Why was it his fault?*

"Nathan," Cole said his name slowly, carefully. "What do you mean, you've gone through what GNAAW left Kiara?"

Nathan ran a frustrated hand through his hair. Of course that's what Cole would focus on, when it was so not the point. "I've just, you know, flipped through it when it was around."

"Did you look for it?"

"I *noticed* it. Noticing something isn't exactly a crime."

"Did you go through Kiara's things, hoping to 'notice' it?"

"No," Nathan said hotly. *Liar, liar.*

"Because that isn't okay, Nathan. You can't snoop through my sister's things. I can't believe I even have to *say* that."

"Would you have shown it to me if I asked?"

"You didn't ask."

"Look, this isn't even the point."

"What is? The fact that you were invited into our home and looked through our stuff? Or the fact that you distrust us—distrust *me*—enough that you felt that was necessary?"

"Oh, my god. You are blowing this out of proportion."

"Am I?"

"Yes!" Nathan shouted. A woman across the street looked over, startled. "Yes," he hissed into the phone,

"We have to talk about this. You can't keep going on this way. It isn't good for you, and it isn't good for us. Or for Dee, by the sound of it."

"Hey, you do not get to bring her into this."

"I didn't bring her into this, Nathan, you did. And really upset her, from the sound of it, by spouting off dubiously acquired information that you were in no position to—"

"Don't you dare lecture me. Dee is my *best friend*. And I'm not going to have her thinking that you all have her back one hundred and ten percent when you don't! When you're lying to her that she's pack! What else are you lying about, Cole? What else have the wolves hidden?"

"Nothing!" Now it was Cole's turn to shout. "You have to stop, Nathan. You're tearing us apart."

Nathan wasn't sure what the "us" was referring to. *Him and Cole, or the pack?* Nathan wasn't sure he wanted to know the answer.

"I thought you were done with this."

"With what?"

"With this fixation on uncovering the truth. There isn't any more truth to uncover. You're going in circles. You need to step back and get some perspective."

"I'm not stepping back."

"Nathan."

"I'm not." Nathan hung up.

Chapter Twenty-Seven

NATHAN FUMED AS HE WALKED down the street. *First Dee, then Cole.* He couldn't understand their resistance to his theory. If werewolves were real, it made sense that they wouldn't be alone! It wasn't as though Nathan was trying to convince them that time travel or, or... aliens existed.

Maybe Cole was right about one thing, though. Nathan had spent the last month with his nose pressed up against the glass of the supernatural world, trying to peer in to see what he could. A break from talking or thinking or fighting with werewolves might be a good thing.

Besides, if he went home right now, he was eighty-percent convinced that Cole would be there, waiting to continue their fight. *Well, fuck that.* Nathan was sick of having to try to prove his point to people who were supposed to support him no matter what.

He shot off a quick text to Isobel and Darren. It was a Friday evening, so they might not be home or they might have other plans. In that case, Nathan would go to a movie or text a non-werewolf friend or find a bar. He'd figure it out. He just needed an escape.

You're more than welcome to come over! Was Darren's quick response, negating Nathan's need for other options.

Awesome, Nathan sent back. **On my way!**

He began to put his phone away and hesitated. He should let someone know where he was going. Even as furious as he was right now, he felt obligated to not just disappear. He pulled up the group chat Dee had set up, which included the two of them and the werewolves, and typed out a message.

Heading out to I&D's. Staying the night. He chewed on his lower lip, debating whether to say something or not about what he suspected Jag was. *Had been. Fuck.* **Watch out for animals being weird. Crows, cats, dogs. Etc.** He didn't care if they believed him or not, he felt responsible to them even when he was pissed. And at least he'd warned them.

Nathan took a left and headed for the bus that would take him to the train out to New Westminster. A night off would be good for him. Give him some perspective. And he was long overdue for a visit with Isobel and Darren.

He hadn't stayed the night in New West since his nightmares had gotten worse and wasn't entirely sure if doing so was a good idea. But he had a joint in his bag, and if he smoked it before falling asleep maybe he'd be fine. And if he wasn't... *oh well.* Nathan would deal with it when it happened. He was exhausted trying to think six steps ahead. He'd meant it when he decided to take the rest of the night off.

Nathan fished his iPod out of his bag and put on his headphones to let the strong beat of Years & Years fill his head and push out everything else.

Chapter Twenty-Eight |

COLE DIDN'T KNOW HOW HIS evening had gotten so turned around. He'd called Nathan to leave a cute message about the little old lady who'd yelled repeatedly "you goddamn assholes" at him and his partner Kate as they'd wheeled her out to their rig, but he'd barely said a word before Nathan had spun them into another fight. He didn't know whether or not to take solace in the fact that Nathan had apparently done the same to Dee.

Cole stopped pacing and dropped into the armchair with his elbows on his knees and his head in his hands. It had been hours since Nathan had hung up on him with no word since his group message—*group message*—that he'd be at his other lovers' home.

Would time with Darren and Isobel give Nathan the step back, the perspective, Cole had suggested he needed? Cole wasn't sure. He just hoped the break did Nathan good.

And what had Nathan meant about watching out for animals acting weird? What was that? Was Nathan going to start going on about werecats now? Weredogs? Cole sighed.

Fuck.

He needed a break. Cole lifted his head and stared bleakly at his living room. For the entire evening after his phone call with Nathan, all he'd been able to picture was Nathan's hands—those long, clever fingers teasing their way into closets and drawers, drawing books from the bookshelves, dragging boxes from under beds. Cole's throat tightened, and he dropped his head again.

Nathan was welcome to make himself at home here. Cole had given Nathan a key. In fact, they all had keys to each other's apartments, except for Ryn. She'd deigned to give Kiara one, but only because Ryn wasn't going to get out of bed to let Kiara out in the mornings, she had claimed. Once he and Nathan began dating, Cole had assumed Nathan understood his implicit permission to feel comfortable in the space.

But there was comfortable, there was making oneself at home, and then there was… what had he said to Nathan? *Snooping. An ugly word. An ugly thing.* And not what he would have expected from Nathan. Maybe he should have. Maybe that was on him.

With a frustrated sigh, Cole stood. He couldn't stay here. He couldn't stand to see his and Kiara's carefully chosen furniture and décor and belongings being rifled through by Nathan's phantom fingers.

Cole stopped in the kitchen long enough to grab a bottle of gin and scrawled a message for Kiara that he left on the table.

Olympic Village was rarely quiet on a summer night, and this was no exception. Despite the late hour, parties had spilled onto balconies, and raucous laughter followed Cole as he wove through the neatly designed buildings and toward False Creek.

It was quieter by the water, though the Village lights glowed behind him, answered by the haze-muffled glow of the lights downtown across the water. Cole strode down the seawall to the small path that connected the tiny patch of land called Beer Island. Because of the connecting path, the land—not even a city block across—wasn't technically an island, and it probably had an official name that wasn't about beer, but Cole had only heard it referred to as Beer Island. That suited him just fine, since the moniker came from its unintended purpose. It was a great place to sit and drink, and that was exactly what Cole planned to do.

Cole headed down the dark path. He let the hold he kept on his senses relax, and the night sounds flooded against him like an embrace: noise from the parties carried on the warm breeze; murmurs of conversation from the handful of people already on the island, who'd had the same idea as Cole; the rustle of the few small animals who called the patch of trees and bush home.

He smelled salt in the city air, mingled with the scent of cheap booze and cigarettes, all secondary to the acrid taste of smoke that suffocated the city.

Cole liked coming here, to the unexpected almost-island that was allowed to run a little wild. He used his supernatural awareness of the humans to take a path through the brush that avoided coming into contact with any of them. On the far side of the island, he dropped down to a few flat boulders only feet above the water.

The distance between Beer Island and downtown Vancouver wasn't great, and on a clear night the lights shone like stars, a glittering invitation that looked close enough to touch. Tonight though, grim haze cast a pall, reflected in the water below, until the whole world seemed encompassed in a globe of smoke. He didn't mind the changed view. It was pretty, in an apocalyptic way.

As the fires in the interior had worsened and more smoke had steadily made its way into the city, Cole had dealt with folks in various stages of respiratory distress. It would only get worse as the haze thickened. It was mean and destructive, but beautiful.

Just like Nathan.

Cole unscrewed the lid from the bottle and took a drink. The gin cut through him like a knife, clean and sharp.

What had he been thinking, to fall for Nathan? The man could barely stay still for five minutes. He was flighty, guarded, and terrified of commitment. He'd only let Cole in reluctantly. Had Cole pushed for too much? Had he backed Nathan into the corner where Nathan was so terrified of finding himself? Or had Nathan imagined the corner and lashed out in panic?

Or was it much simpler than that? Cole was a werewolf. Nathan had only learned of their existence a year ago. Would that simple fact be the insurmountable wedge that drove them apart?

Too many factors. Too many questions. Cole took another drink. He was a fool, to think this relationship would work. *Better to ignore Nathan's passes. Find himself a nice, stable werewolf boy.* He could be on GNAAW's dating app now, having his choice of men who'd take Cole's existence as a given and not the first piece in a much larger puzzle.

Ah. That was it, then. The part that stung the most, that was the base of the hard, deep hurt Cole nursed tonight in his gut. He was worried that Nathan looked at him and only saw the wolf.

Well, and why shouldn't I be? Cole took another bitter drink. *For a person who prized novelty as much as Nathan did, what was more novel than a werewolf?*

A murder, apparently.

Cole had spent these last months with Nathan imagining a future together: a house, kids, maybe. Cole wanted a garden. He'd allowed that dream to grow, and all the while Nathan had been fixated on the "and then what?" question Cole's existence posed. *No, not even his. Theirs. It wasn't Cole that had sent Nathan off on his goose chase, it was werewolves, period.*

Idiot, he chastised himself. Every ounce of common sense had told him to stay far away from Nathan, and what had Cole done? Thrown himself in head first, with no thought as to whether Nathan had followed.

He guessed he deserved to be where he was now. Cole took another drink and stared moodily into the haze.

THE SUDDEN, ORANGE FLARE OF her cigarette alerted him. Cole glanced to his left to see Kiara leaning casually against the rocks. Alpha-designate of their father's pack growing up, and Alpha of her own pack now, Cole's younger sister could move with enough skill and silence that she could, in fact, sneak up on another werewolf.

She took a drag from her slender cigarette and held out her hand expectantly for the bottle. Saying nothing, Cole passed it over.

She lifted it up, took a swig, made a face as she gave it back, and wiped her mouth with the back of her hand. Kiara was a tequila drinker.

"Don't we have enough smoke?" Cole asked dryly, as she took another drag.

"Yeah, but this is menthol."

Cole rolled his eyes and looked out over the water. Kiara took a seat closer to him, and for a few minutes they just sat. Cole took an occasional drink of the gin—he could feel it now, the buzz of it in his veins—and Kiara lit a second cigarette.

"It does bug you then," she said finally.

"What?"

"Nathan. His... extracurriculars."

It took Cole a minute to figure out that she wasn't referring to Nathan's obsession with the supernatural, but the fact that Nathan was poly.

"No," he said, surprised. "No, I have no problem with him seeing other people. He's been with Darren and Isobel for longer than he's been with me," he reminded Kiara.

She shot him a look. "You're not weirded out at all that he's with them right now? He's there and you're here." She gestured at the island, at the half-drunk bottle of gin. "And that's just fine for you?"

Cole shrugged. He wasn't sure Kiara, who was possessive with her friends and family, let alone her lover, could understand. "I love him." *True, even now.* Would be true, in any tragic future Cole could imagine. And over the course of the night he'd imagined many of them. "I don't own him. I don't want to own him."

"Right, but," Kiara persisted, plucking the gin from Cole's fingers. "Don't you want other lovers as well, then? I mean... even if you really don't care, doesn't this feel a bit one-sided?"

"I don't want other lovers." Cole sighed and tipped his head back. "I just want Nathan. I want a future with him," he admitted. "I want that. I want decades. I want to grow old together. I'm not like Nathan; I don't need a lot of people. I only need one." And that was Nathan.

As a gay man, non-monogamy was hardly brand-new to Cole. He had no real preference for or against it, but was content to be with the person he was with when he was with them and happy for them to do as they pleased when they weren't together.

Nathan took his freedom seriously, and Cole respected that, admired it. Nathan had been clear from the beginning that he had no interest in a traditional relationship, and if that had been a deal breaker for Cole, he would have ended things then—or not started them.

Kiara shook her head. "I don't get it."

"And I don't get how you and Ryn can be at each other's throats as often as you are and still stay together. How do you stomach it? This is awful." Cole grimaced.

"Hah." It was Kiara's turn to give a graceless shrug. "I like it. I like that Ryn isn't afraid of me, or intimidated by me, or impressed by me. She'll go toe-to-toe with me any day of the week, no question. And we know what we are to each other. I'm trying, this time, to make sure she knows. We both are. When you're secure like that…" She locked her hands together. "…it keeps you steady."

Cole pointed at her with the neck of the rapidly emptying bottle. "Exactly. That's how me and Nathan are." He mimicked her locked hands. "So he can do what he wants, and I can do what I want, but when it comes down to it, we're this." He held up his locked hands. "Or… we were. I thought we were. I don't know. I'm wondering now, was it ever me he was attracted to, or the idea of me? A *werewolf*." Cole snorted with derision.

"Hey." Kiara gripped his shoulder. Unwilling to meet her gaze, Cole looked at the water at their feet. "In case you forget, Nathan did have at least one other werewolf to choose from—two, if you count Jamie, though I doubt he would have. Three, when you add Ryn to the mix! He picked you. Werewolf or no, he picked you for this." She poked a finger at Cole's chest, right above his heart.

"If it was only the excitement he wanted, trust me, there were better bets than you, my brother."

Cole shrugged self-consciously. "He's looking for something more interesting."

"No," Kiara corrected. "He's had his whole world turned upside down and he's trying to make sense of it. That's all. He's lost all sense of control, and he thinks if he can discover the next bump in the road before it discovers him, he'll have that control back."

Cole stared at her, one eyebrow raised. "That's… quite the insight."

Kiara grabbed the bottle and took a drink, avoiding Cole's gaze. "We're alike. Sometimes. I kinda get what he's going through. It's hard to lose control."

"I know how to pick 'em, I guess." Cole knocked his shoulder into Kiara's companionably.

"Shut up."

"At least I'm nothing like Ryn."

"Can we go back to not talking?"

"Oh, that's not true, we both like *Parks and Rec*."

"And you're both assholes."

Chapter Twenty-Nine |

NATHAN WOKE SLOWLY, ALMOST UNWILLING to open his eyes, he was so comfortable. Isobel and Darren had made up the guest room for him, and Nathan wasn't sure whether it was the change of scenery, the change of company, or a whole night spent without one mention of anything werewolf-related or supernatural weirdness, but he'd slept straight through till morning.

Of course, it could have been the sex. And the joint split with Darren after had probably helped.

Either way, Nathan never wanted to leave. He snuggled deeper into the white bedding. He didn't have his glasses on and couldn't make out the time on the clock on the bedside table, but the light streaming from behind the drapes said it was probably mid-morning.

He didn't want to get up. He really didn't want to get up. If he got up, he'd have to face the real world again, and the real world involved at least four people, most of whom were werewolves, who'd be mad at him.

Nathan groaned and rolled over.

"You're up." Isobel's voice floated in from the hallway, warm and amused.

"I'm not," Nathan insisted. He twisted his neck so he could see her standing in the open doorway, wrapped in her favorite purple robe with her hair haloed in a soft Afro around her head.

"Come down when you are. Darren is making pancakes, and they should be ready soon."

Pancakes. Maybe he wouldn't have to face the real world quite yet. Luxuriating in the soft bed, Nathan closed his eyes for another few minutes before he forced himself to get up.

He didn't bother with pants, just yanked on the T-shirt he'd worn yesterday and went downstairs in his boxers and bare feet.

Darren stood flipping pancakes at the stove wearing nothing but an apron. Isobel handed Nathan a cup of coffee and gave him a kiss.

"Mmm, morning," Nathan said. He took a sip of coffee and wandered over to Darren. Darren smirked when Nathan's hand ghosted over the curve of Darren's bare ass that peeked out at the open back of the apron.

"Morning," Darren murmured. He turned his face so Nathan could kiss him too.

"This is great." Nathan took a seat at the table and settled back. "Remind me why I ever leave?"

"Because you get squirrely in the suburbs. And you'd hate the commute into work each day," Isobel reminded him.

"True." Nathan helped himself to the first batch of steaming pancakes when Darren set them on the table. The pancakes were perfect, round, golden, and fluffy enough that Nathan almost felt bad as he cut into one. He took a bite and moaned. "You two are great. Thanks for the last-minute date last night. I'm glad you were both free."

"Us, too." Isobel took her own seat and reached for the Saskatoon berry syrup, which matched the deep purple of her robe.

"You sleep well?" Darren brought the second batch of pancakes to the table and joined them.

"So good," Nathan said around a mouthful of pancake. "Best sleep I've had in weeks."

Darren and Isobel traded looks. "Is there something going on with you? We aren't trying to pry, but you, well, you don't look great."

"Hey!" Nathan frowned at Darren. "I didn't hear you complaining last night."

Isobel and Darren traded looks again. "You just look worn down," Isobel explained. "Is everything okay with you and Cole?"

"God." Nathan pushed back from the table—reluctantly, because he was really enjoying Darren's pancakes. "Not everything is about Cole, all right? I have my own stuff."

"We know." Isobel caught his hand. "Hang on. Take a breath. We only ask because we care about you, okay? We don't have to talk about it if you don't want to. But we…" She gestured to herself and her husband. "…are here for you. You know that, right?" She squeezed his hand.

"Yeah." Nathan relaxed back into his chair and picked up his fork. "I'm fine. Everything is fine. I'm having trouble sleeping sometimes. That's it."

"Well, Nathan…" Darren held Nathan's gaze, his dark eyes kind. "You found a body, a really brutally murdered body not that long ago. It would stand to reason that you are struggling. Have you talked to anyone about it?"

"Talked to—what, you mean like a therapist?"

Darren nodded. "Or a counselor. There are people, trained professionals, who can help you work through trauma."

Right, as if Nathan could walk into a therapist's office, plunk himself down on the couch, and announce that, ever since he'd discovered werewolves existed, he's been pretty sure things other than werewolves existed, too, though his werewolf boyfriend disagreed. Oh, and he'd found the body of what he was pretty sure was one of those other things, but no one would believe him. So, between that, getting nearly killed himself by a werewolf a year ago, and then being held hostage and knocked around by an also-secret group of human werewolf hunters, he was having a rough time.

Maybe the therapist would prescribe him anti-psychotics or maybe he'd find himself committed.

Nathan fought to keep a lid on his temper. Isobel and Darren didn't know any of that. The only recent changes in his life, as far as they were aware, was the introduction of Cole and the discovery of Jag's body. He couldn't fault them for their concern, considering the state he found himself in.

"The detective gave me the number for a counselor." It wasn't even a lie; Nathan still had the card somewhere. "Maybe you're right. Maybe I should give them a call." That part was a lie, but it wasn't as if Nathan could tell them the truth—and if he ignored what was, in any other scenario, pretty strong advice, they'd have more cause to worry.

"I think that's a great idea." Isobel smiled at him and Darren.

"It is," Nathan agreed, touching his bare foot to Darren's bare calf under the table. "Thank you," he said sincerely. The advice was well-meant, even if it was wildly inapplicable.

"You can thank me by going," Darren responded.

Nathan pushed another bite of pancake into his mouth and forced a smile.

Chapter Thirty

NATHAN WAS LATER GETTING HOME from Isobel and Darren's than he'd planned to be. But they'd talked him into seeing *Atomic Blonde* with them, and as Nathan hadn't had a chance to see it yet, he was hard pressed to say no. It had been so nice to sit in a theatre and watch a movie without worrying about any unscheduled werewolf interruptions, that Nathan had been able to relax. And despite the suggested-therapy hiccup over breakfast, Nathan came back from the visit refreshed. It had been good to spend time being normal, and he'd missed Isobel's wicked humor and Darren's thoughtful smile. And the luxury of a full night's sleep could not be overstated.

He felt more present in his own skin than he had in days. One of his favorite things about being poly and dating many people was that it forced him to know himself. He couldn't fall into a rut with someone, conform himself to fit them, and simply grow that way from then on. He had to be firmly himself or he'd lose himself trying to fit so many other people.

And what an identity I've managed, Nathan thought wryly. He'd pissed off the two people closest to him.

And he wished he hadn't. But he needed to trust himself; he was all he had. He had to trust himself or he couldn't trust anything. So that's what he was doing, trusting himself. And it sucked that doing so put him at odds with Dee and with Cole. But Nathan didn't know what else to do.

He trudged from the train toward his apartment. Smoke still hung over the city, glowing Halloween-orange from the reflected streetlights. The hair pricked on Nathan's nape. He'd had his headphones in when he walked out of the station, but now yanked them out of his ears and hooked them in the collar of his shirt. He felt muffled enough.

He turned the corner to his apartment, uncomfortably aware of the slap of his sneakers against the pavement. Though Nathan hadn't thought it was very late, the smoke cast a pall of false twilight. The street ahead of him was deserted.

Before to this last year, one of Nathan's favorite things about his neighborhood was its slow transformation from industrial warehouses to residential. Nathan's apartment was one of the first buildings to be converted.

The solitude no longer seemed charming, but chilling, which was ridiculous. He was in the middle of the city, and, in a city the size of Vancouver, that was saying something. It was hardly as though Nathan was still on the outskirts of a prairie town.

Or, was it? Nathan's skin was hot to the touch. While the haze kept the glare of the sun away, it also trapped muggy heat that clung in a thick film. Despite the heat, a chill worked its way up Nathan's spine.

The smoke was presumably from the forest fires. *But was it? The smoke, plus the bird, plus the cat Arthur and Jamie had encountered, plus a murdered sorcerer. Who knew how the world would react to something like that?* If Jag had ties to nature, was Nathan experiencing the aftereffects of his death?

Nathan rubbed his bare arms and kept his eyes open wide as he approached his building. Someone was coming toward him on the other side of the street. Under the heavy shadow of the trees that lined the block, Nathan couldn't make out anything but the heavy tread of their steps.

Nathan's heart pounded, and he grabbed about in his bag for his keys. The person began to cross the street. Nathan found his keys, closed his fingers over the metal and pulled them out. He looked up, and the keys dropped to the sidewalk with a clatter.

A two-headed dog, half in shadow, walked in front of the man. Terror froze Nathan's entire body. For an immobile moment that stretched into eternity, Nathan was certain that he was about to die, devoured by two slavering jaws and digested into their shared stomach. And then the dog moved out of shadow, split into two German Shepherds of nearly equal height.

"Evening," the man said, as he and his dogs passed. Nathan managed a jerky nod; his limbs weakened to noodles when the man turned the corner. He bent down and picked up his keys and balled them in his fist until the metal edges cut in deep enough to hurt.

He could still taste his heart in his throat, a meaty copper pulse. He had to figure out what he was up against. He had to find out what Jag had been, so he'd know how to keep everyone safe. He hadn't known about werewolves, and one had nearly gotten Dee. He hadn't known about the Huntsmen, and they *had* gotten him, and very nearly Ryn as well.

If he found out first this time, they wouldn't be caught so unawares.

Nathan let himself into the building and gave the garbage and recycling room a wide berth as he crossed to the elevator.

Chapter Thirty-One

IT WAS THREE DAYS AFTER his fights with Dee and Cole, and Nathan had yet to hear a word from either of them.

The group chat remained silent. Ryn had sent a peace-sign-hand emoji in response to Nathan's message to watch out for weird animals, and that had been that.

Nathan had debated texting his best friend and his boyfriend, but the thought of having to "talk" about Friday held him off. *What would be the point, considering neither of them believed him?* No, Nathan would wait until he had more information, if not confirmation, about Jag—which Nathan was certain he was about to discover.

If any part of him had hoped that his evening with Isobel and Darren had broken the spell of insomnia, it had been wrong. Instead of sleeping, Nathan had put the night to good use. Thanks to the brilliance of the Internet, he'd spent the night watching YouTube videos about how to pick a lock.

He'd watched for hours and practiced the movements with his hands until he could mimic the video without looking at the screen. Then, once it was late enough that he was sure his neighbors would be asleep, he'd crept out into the hallway at three-thirty a.m. and spent two hours practicing on his own door.

By the time the sun was rising and he had to get back inside before someone spotted him and asked what the hell he was doing, Nathan was able to unlock his own door in under a minute.

Then he'd slept, long and deep and dreamless. If he hadn't made sure to set a wakeup alarm for one-thirty p.m., Nathan might have slept the day right through.

As it was, he'd gotten out of bed, showered, dressed, and was now cautiously climbing the stairs to Jag's floor.

His initial instinct had been to break in—*no, not break in, to visit*—Jag's apartment on Sunday, but it had occurred to Nathan that most people had Sundays off and were likely to be in and out of their apartments all day. This was not the best time to enter one of those apartments through dubious means and unobserved.

So he'd readjusted his plans and Sunday night had emailed his boss to let her know that he wasn't feeling well and probably wouldn't be in on Monday.

He figured most people in his building worked a nine-to-five job the way he did. There were bound to be a few who worked from home, or did shift work like Cole, but Nathan spent a chunk of his Sunday trying to figure out what time of day his building was apt to be the most deserted and decided on two p.m.

Office workers would probably still be at the office. Given the hot, though still hazy, summer afternoon, people who worked from home were probably out enjoying the summer day or running errands. As for anyone else, Nathan would be quick.

He reached Jag's floor and peeked through the stair door's narrow window. The hallway was deserted. Nathan checked his watch: three minutes after two. He wanted to be in Jag's apartment by two-fifteen at the latest so that he could get out of there by three-fifteen. He didn't want make his way out of Jag's apartment and back to his own when people started getting home from work.

Nathan let out a slow breath, trying to calm the nerves that made his palms slick with sweat. He hadn't left room in his timeline for dawdling. It was now or never.

You got this, he told himself. He'd watched a million videos. He'd practiced for hours. He put more effort in learning how to pick a lock than he'd ever spent on piano lessons. *You got this.*

He approached Jag's door, 408. If there'd been police tape across it, it had been taken down. In fact, nothing marked Jag's door as being different than any other on this floor. Nathan wasn't sure why he'd expected otherwise.

"You got this." Nathan pulled his lock-picking tools from his pocket: a pair of Deanna's bobby pins that he was always finding in his couch or in his bathroom, which he'd bent as the video showed him.

"Nathan, is that you?"

He leapt back from the door as if it was on fire, spinning to face Emily with his hand that held the pins hidden behind his back.

"Emily, hey." Nathan gave a weak smile. The initial rush of adrenaline at being caught red-handed faded, and he felt exhausted. "How's it going?"

"Fine." She looked at him curiously and gestured at an apartment farther down the hall, closer to the elevator. "That's me. I was just heading out for a walk." She gave a wan smile. "I'm trying to get some work done, but I'm not focusing." She shrugged self-consciously. "Hoping a walk will help."

"Oh? Yeah. Neat." *Neat.* What the fuck was that? "I, um…" Nathan's carefully prepared excuse floundered on his tongue, undone by Emily's tired hazel eyes. "I wanted to see Jag's apartment," Nathan admitted.

"You feel a connection with him now." Emily said it matter-of-factly, and Nathan was surprised to find that he didn't disagree.

"Yeah." *Maybe not a connection the way Emily was thinking, but a connection nonetheless.*

"Come on." Emily took a small crystal keychain from her purse. "He'd have me water his plants when he went away. I have a key."

"Are, uh, are you sure?" Now that he was about to enter through licit means, Nathan felt a thousand times worse. Emily was prepared to let him in out of the goodness of her heart, and Nathan had been ready and willing to break in. *And for what, really? To satisfy his curiosity? To prove a point?*

Emily was proof positive that whatever else Jag had been, he had also been a regular dude to a lot of people: a friend who asked a neighbor to water his plants, a guy who, like Nathan, had plants that needed watering. *Did it matter, really, if Jag was anything else on top of that?*

Yes, Nathan's mind insisted. *Just because Jag is a friendly sorcerer doesn't mean that the next one will be too. Or the one after that. Or the one after that. You need to be* prepared.

Emily held open the door and gestured Nathan through.

Chapter Thirty-Two |

THE FIRST THING NATHAN NOTICED were the plants. Nathan had plants—lots of people had plants. But there was having plants, and then there was *having plants*.

Vancouver was technically in a rainforest, but to prairie-boy Nathan—whose understanding of what a rainforest looked like came primarily from *FernGully*—it rarely seemed like being in a rainforest. Jag's apartment, on the other hand, was like being plunked down in the cartoon version—the hip, urban one. Greenery, in pots and terrariums large and small, seemed to take over the apartment. But after the initial shock of so many plants in a relatively small space, Nathan could pick out the details of the apartment.

Jag's apartment was laid out like Nathan's own, but with a few jarring tweaks. Jag's kitchen was on the other side than his—though his stairs to the second level were still on the right. Instead of Nathan's island, Jag had a kitchen table and chairs. Nathan had a split second of dizzy double-vision, seeing his own apartment laid over Jag's.

"That's a lot of plants to water," Nathan remarked.

Emily gave a rueful laugh. "I know. But I didn't mind. He always left good instructions."

"He lived alone?" It occurred to Nathan that he did not know the answer. He'd been planning to break into an apartment that might have had someone inside.

Yikes.

"Just him," Emily confirmed. "I keep thinking; what if I'd been there, you know?"

"Do they know any more about who killed him? Or why?"

Emily shook her head. Obviously at home in the space, she wandered to the living room and sank into an armchair tucked beside a leafy fern. "They still haven't found his head. Or his hands." Her chin wobbled as she blinked away tears.

"I'm sorry," Nathan said and meant it.

"Thanks." She sniffed audibly. "What is it you wanted to see?"

"I—" *His secret sorcerer shit. Tails of newt. Mystery potion. His scrying bowl. You know, the usual.* "Um." Nathan cast about for something that made sense. "I don't know." *His magic garden of plants with supernatural properties.* "I just... I mean..."

"It's not something specific." Emily nodded. "I get it."

"Yeah. I just kind of want to get a sense of him. Who he was." *There. Not even really a lie.*

Emily waved an open hand at the apartment. "Take your time. I don't really feel much like a walk now."

She toyed with the seat cushion. "His parents are coming to pack up his things next week. I'll help, and some of his other friends."

"Me, too." Nathan surprised himself with his offer. "I mean, I can help, also, if it's okay." He wanted to. He owed it, a little, to Jag.

"Thank you." Emily's eyes welled with tears again. "That's just like him, you know, Jag. He always had people wanting to be around him."

Nathan froze on his way up the stairs—which were dotted with tiny pots and budding green things. *Was his desire to help genuine, or was he under a spell right now? Was he here of his own volition? Was the glamour Jag cast still potent after his death? Was it more potent?*

Emily rose to follow Nathan up the stairs, and Nathan forced his wooden limbs to move.

Jag's bedroom was laid out with his bed facing the stairs, as opposed to Nathan's who'd tucked his in on the right wall. Jag had a large closet there, and beside a single bookshelf on the left-hand side stood a sturdy wooden chest. A few plants were suspended in baskets from the ceiling and attached to the wall behind his bed. Another cascaded leaves down the side of the bookshelf.

"For such a sociable guy, it's kinda weird that he lived alone. No girlfriend? Boyfriend? Enbyfriend?"

"No. He… he…"

Nathan paid attention with half an ear; his eyes darted everywhere. After so long imagining it, being finally surrounded with Jag's stuff was almost overwhelming. If he was under a spell, one that had survived its creator's death, he probably needed to find the physical object it was tied to. His fingers itched to open the chest. *Who the hell even owned a chest in 2017? And that was another new, interesting question to consider—how old had Jag been?* The chest looked ancient. If Nathan could just get Emily to go downstairs, he was certain he'd—

Emily's gasping sob yanked his attention back to her.

"He had a party last month, and we were really drunk, and he— we—kissed. He said he loved me. I said—" Emily broke into another sob. "I said I'd have to think about it. Travis was pushing me to move in with him, but we'd been rocky, and Jag was so wonderful. I had to think. I didn't know what I felt, I didn't know what to do. So I had to take some time, except now he's *dead* and now I'll never know." She turned her tear-streaked face up to him. "What if I loved him?"

Shit.

Chapter Thirty-Three |

"IT'S OKAY, YOU COULDN'T HAVE known." Nathan rubbed his hand soothingly over Emily's back as she sobbed into his chest. He had exactly zero idea what he was supposed to do or say. He had not seen the curveball love triangle of Emily, Jag, and Travis coming. *Was it a love spell?* Emily said she wasn't sure how she'd felt about Jag, but now she was crying about him in Nathan's arms—what if she was caught up like Nathan, but without any idea of what might be going on?

Nathan brought his hands down to grip her shoulders and took a step back so he could look her in the eye. He'd have to come clean. She deserved to know—and she could help him look for the charms that held the spells.

"Emily," he began. A sharp knock on the door downstairs interrupted him.

Nathan frowned, and Emily stepped out of his grip. She pressed her hands to her face, wiping away her tears as best she could. "I'd better get that." She smiled halfheartedly and went back down the stairs.

Who'd be knocking on Jag's door? And how had they gotten into the building? Visitors needed to be buzzed up. Shit. What if it was the police? They must have an override code. Nathan had been found with the body and now he was creeping around Jag's apartment. *Was there any way they'd release him a second time?*

"Emily, wait." Nathan started forward a moment too late, as he heard Emily unlock and open the door.

"Travis." Her voice seemed surprised. "What are you doing here?"

"What are *you* doing here?"

The door closed. From upstairs, Nathan couldn't see what was happening. Should he go down?

"I was just showing Nathan around. And," Emily added hurriedly, "I wanted to water Jag's plants."

"You need to let go of your attachment to this place. I'm sure his family appreciates you keeping an eye on it until they can get here, but it's not your responsibility, Emily. You have enough on your plate already," Travis chided. His voice sharpened with his next words. "You said that guy Nathan is here?"

And that was his cue. Nathan popped his head over the half-wall of the second floor and waved down. "Hey."

Travis stepped into the living room and looked up. Emily trailed behind him with one arm hugged across her chest.

"Emily, I don't think you should be hanging around this guy. Didn't you say he's the one you found with Jag's body?"

Nathan straightened, affronted.

Travis's voice lowered so that Nathan had to strain to hear his next words. "I thought he didn't know Jag; why would he want to be in his apartment?"

Whoa. Okay. This was rapidly spiraling out of Nathan's control. He eased back from the ledge and, holding his hands carefully empty at his sides, came down the stairs. *See? Harmless.*

"I just wished I knew him better, that's all. But I'm probably done here, so, Emily, why don't we…" Nathan jerked a thumb at the front door.

"It's pretty weird, you being here." Travis moved to stand between Nathan, Emily, and the door. "I don't know if I can just let you leave."

"Excuse me?"

"Travis!"

"Look, Emily, you know I love how trusting you are, but sometimes you're too trusting. Who knows what this guy was really doing? What evidence he's already destroyed?"

"What *evidence* I—" Nathan spluttered. "I haven't destroyed any evidence." His palms started to sweat. He hadn't even touched anything. Travis was throwing a wrench into Nathan's entire plan.

"I think we should let the police sort that out." Travis reached into his pocket and pulled out his phone. "Emily, baby, why don't you come stand here behind me."

"Oh, come on." Nathan dismissed Travis and switched his focus to Emily. "Emily, I was telling you the truth." *Kinda.* "I'm not trying to destroy any evidence. I didn't kill Jag. I didn't even know him!"

Emily stood between them. Her eyes were red from crying, and she bit her bottom lip. "Travis, I don't think he's lying. He's having a rough time, like me, and that's it."

"Are you sure?" Travis lifted an eyebrow. "How much do you really know about this guy?"

"Hey." Nathan lifted his hands and held them out in front of him, placating. "I'm a librarian. I work at the university. I live on the floor below. I'm a lot of things, but a murderer isn't one of them." How had his life got so twisted that now he was trying to convince someone of that simple fact? "Seriously. I just want to get out of your hair." *Let me go.*

It wasn't as though Travis was holding him there, not exactly. But Travis's broad shoulders seemed to fill the small hallway from the kitchen to the door, and there was no mistaking the aggression in Travis's stance. Nathan was seventy percent sure that if he tried to leave, Travis would move. But the leftover thirty percent of him wasn't so sure. And if that happened, if Travis didn't get out of his way, Nathan had no idea what his next move would be. That uncertainty held him.

"Travis, this is ridiculous. Nathan didn't kill Jag."

"Who did, then, Emily? Who killed your best buddy? Who cut off his head? Who took his hands?" Travis's words were barbed, and Emily flinched as each one landed. "'Everyone loves Jag'," Travis mimicked in a high-pitched approximation of Emily's voice. "Someone obviously didn't. You've always been too soft-hearted, Emily. You always want to see the best in everyone. First Jag, now this guy." He jerked his head toward Nathan.

"Don't talk about him like that!" Emily's face was flushed. Nathan would be touched, but he knew her concern wasn't for him, but Jag.

"Hey, I'm not trying to insult the dead." Travis shrugged. "I'm only saying he wasn't as great as you think he was. And, if I'm being honest, maybe now that he's gone you won't have such a strong tie to this place." He gestured to the hallway behind them, presumably indicating Emily's apartment. "That isn't such a bad thing."

"This does not sound like a conversation I need to be a part of." Nathan inched toward the door. There was enough room between Travis and the kitchen table that he thought he could sneak through without having to ask Travis to move. "So, I'm just gonna go…" He felt a little bad leaving Emily. But her asshole boyfriend wasn't Nathan's responsibility. Though he would definitely have a talk with her about what respectful, healthy communication was like.

"No." Travis turned into Nathan's space as he tried to move past. Nathan took a hasty step back and knocked into one of the kitchen chairs.

"Look, Travis, I'm not trying to start anything here, all right? I'm just going to go back to my apartment. We can forget this whole thing ever happened." Nathan's heart raced. He reminded himself that he faced down angry werewolves on a regular basis. Travis was nothing compared to Kiara—except three times her size and without her sense of honor or control.

"By *this whole thing* do you mean you luring my girlfriend into the apartment of the man you killed?"

"What? No! Dude. Come on." Nathan shook his head, dismayed. "All I wanted was to see it, and Emily kindly helped me out. That's it. We just got here, anyway." It had certainly not been enough time for Nathan to poke around the way he had planned. An image of the chest upstairs flashed in his mind. He'd come back tonight, when he was sure he'd be alone. *Two's company, three's a crowd. Which, hang on*— "Why are *you* here?" he asked, eyes narrowing.

"I was looking for Emily."

Emily frowned. "How'd you know I'd be here?"

Travis lifted his shoulder in a careless shrug. "Lucky guess."

Nathan doubted that.

"You know what?" Travis fixed Nathan with his gaze. "I think you were right; you should go."

Right, now that Nathan was questioning Travis's presence it was okay for him to go. Nathan suddenly felt very strongly that he should stay. He hadn't liked Travis after meeting him in the grocery store, and now dislike tumbled rapidly into unease.

Nathan stood, torn. He wasn't comfortable leaving Emily with Travis, but he was equally unsure as to whether his continued presence would make the situation worse.

"Actually, Travis," Emily said. "I think *you* should go. Nathan and I are almost done here, and, as much as I appreciate you stopping by, I don't think I'm really up for company tonight." She smiled as she said it, but the smile didn't quite reach her eyes.

"You want me to go?" Disbelief rang in Travis's voice.

Emily nodded. "It's been a long day, and we'll be out of here soon anyway." She moved closer to the two of them and touched Travis's forearm. "I'll call you tomorrow, okay?"

Travis looked down where her fingers rested against his skin. He shook her off. "You were crying."

"What?" Emily's hand flew to her face. "No. I mean—yes. It's hard being back here. That's all." She seemed to deflate.

"Is it?" Travis asked.

"Yeah," Nathan butted in sharply. "It is. She was sad because her friend died. Try to show a little sympathy."

Travis's focus returned to Nathan. "Why are you still here?"

"Why are you such a dick?"

Travis's nostrils flared. "You're gonna want to be careful how you talk to me."

"Or what?" Nathan's anger and stress boiled over. He was supposed to be trying to figure out some supernatural shit and instead he was stuck taking verbal swipes at this meathead. "You'll just keep being a dick? Sorry, I'm over it." He pushed past Travis. Travis moved faster than Nathan anticipated and flung Nathan back. Nathan hit the kitchen chair and they both toppled to the floor.

Chapter Thirty-Four |

Cole stood gratefully in the shower after his shift. The water pounded against his shoulders, and he tilted his head back into the spray. It had been a long day. The haze remained, and emergency calls continued to rise. It was the fourth day in a row without sun or sky or clouds, and the sensation of being trapped had gone from itchy to suffocating.

Cole had long practice at ignoring or tuning out his wolf senses. He struggled, though, with the smoke. The air was heavy with it. Even now, under the damp steam of the shower, Cole could smell the burning mountainsides. It instilled an insistent, low-key panic at the base of his spine, one he'd carried with him all day: an instinct to flee.

His head throbbed. The tension headache had started only hours into his work shift and had worsened. As a werewolf, he healed at a quicker rate than a human; headaches weren't often a problem. The effort it took to keep his senses closed down, to shut out the smoke, and to do his job as though nothing was wrong had taken a toll. Add the insistent, throbbing pain of his brain on top of that, and Cole was miserable.

He turned his face into the water, letting the pressure and the heat smooth away as much of his tension as it could. He'd been at work well before the sun rose, and all he wanted was to be able to crawl straight into bed. Washing off the sweat and the grime had seemed like a good idea fifteen minutes ago, but now that Cole was naked and clean he wanted to be able to fall straight into bed.

He'd have to turn off the shower, get dressed, and drive there first. Cole stood under the water for another minute, letting his hands hang limply by his sides as he soaked in as much relaxation as he could.

Unless he wanted to be here until his shift started tomorrow, he had to go. Cole reluctantly turned off the shower and grabbed his towel. He dried off and made his way to his locker. He was glad he had shorts and a loose cotton tank top to wear.

He waved at a pair of coworkers who were starting their shift and jogged down the stairs to the parking lot.

The sky was the same featureless gray it had been all day. Driving home, Cole's fingers tapped on the wheel. Nathan had gone dark again—nothing after his message Friday night. Cole tried to hang on to his anger, his indignation, but under his own hurt was the certainty that Nathan was hurting too. Cole wished he knew what to do, what to say, how to help. It would be easier if he could just stay angry. He had every right to be. But he'd felt Nathan's terror on the nights Nathan had woken up screaming. He'd witnessed the fear that Nathan fought so hard to keep at bay.

Nathan was doing the best he could. *Was it really his fault, if his best sucked for everyone around him?*

Yes, a cranky part of Cole insisted. Cole sighed. It wouldn't be so bad if there was an end in sight, some reasonable time frame for Nathan to process whatever he was going through. But this impossible, unknowable conflict loomed large, and Cole wasn't sure what it would take to fix it.

He only knew he had to try.

At a stoplight, Cole dropped his forehead against his hand on the steering wheel. He'd go home. It was only just after two now. He'd sleep for a couple hours. Then he'd go to Nathan's. It was unlikely Nathan would go out on a Monday night, and, though Cole didn't love the idea of a second, unannounced visit, he had to admit that his first one had gone over well enough.

Besides, if Nathan didn't want visitors he could damn well say as much. Then again, that would force him to actually communicate, and god knew, for someone who had no trouble running his mouth, Nathan clammed up at the most inconvenient times.

Maybe Cole would text this time first.

The light turned green, and Cole drove. He'd figure it out when he woke up. Right now he needed the kind oblivion of sleep and, he was reminded as his stomach growled, something to eat.

Chapter Thirty-Five |

"TRAVIS!" EMILY'S HORRIFIED VOICE FOLLOWED the crash of Nathan into the chair, and then the chair and Nathan onto the floor. Nathan's arms moved sluggishly as his brain tried to catch up with the reality of his body. Pain was always shocking and never more so than when it was delivered intentionally by another person.

"No, enough of this, Emily. You keep finding these mediocre guys to befriend, and I'm tired of it. Whatever you see in this guy." Travis jerked his thumb at Nathan struggling on the floor. "Whatever you saw in Jag, it's ridiculous." He blew out an incredulous laugh. "And, you know, even with all of that—I did not see this still happening." He circled his finger to indicate Jag's apartment. "The guy is dead. Move on. More importantly, move *in*."

"Oh, my god, Travis. Nathan, are you okay?"

"Are you even listening to me? That guy doesn't matter. Nathan, Jag, they don't matter. They're distractions."

Emily knelt beside Nathan and helped him to sit.

Nathan's glasses had stayed on his face this time. *Why was it that people were always hitting him?* His mouth, Kiara would probably say.

He flinched when Travis reached down, but it wasn't Nathan Travis hauled up, but Emily. She yelped, and Nathan scrambled unsteadily to his feet after her.

"Let her go," he told Travis. Travis's grip was tight on Emily's arm and digging into the fabric of her shirt.

Travis ignored Nathan as though he wasn't even in the room. He shook Emily. "You and me, Emily, that's what matters. That's the focus, okay? Now I think we can both agree that this building isn't a good space for you to be in. It's just not."

As Travis continued to talk—about his condo in Yaletown, of all things—Nathan shifted his body so that his butt was angled away from Travis. With a wary eye on the other man, he slowly brought one of his own hands behind his back and began to inch his phone from his pocket.

Nathan was moderately hopeful that he could dial 911 without looking. Upside down. With his hand behind his back.

"You're hurting me."

Nathan's attention snapped back to Emily. Silent tears ran down her face. Nathan let a slow breath out through his nose. After a year spent with werewolves, it seemed almost ludicrous that Nathan had no recourse against Travis. He was used to his furry pals tackling bad guys—a knockdown, drag out fight where his side vastly outmatched the other side.

Nathan stood zero chance against Travis in a one-to-one fight, and he wouldn't lay odds on him and Emily being able to do defend themselves together, either.

"I'm sorry, babe." Travis's grip appeared to relax fractionally. "I'm only trying to show you how your choices hurt me. I want us to move forward."

If Nathan had a weapon, that might make things different. But all he had was his phone. And he'd just about pulled it free of his pocket.

Chapter Thirty-Six |

COLE GOT UP FROM HIS restless bed less than an hour after he'd gotten into it. Despite the weariness heavy in his shoulders, and the food in his belly, he couldn't settle. His thoughts returned, again and again, to Nathan. From what Jamie had said, the fight he'd had with Deanna was still unresolved. Cole couldn't imagine Nathan was dealing well with that.

He couldn't imagine Nathan dealing well with anything right now. Cole fought not to feel responsible, not responsible for Nathan's meltdown, but for Nathan's care, for not being there, for not helping when he so desperately wanted to.

His head was a mess.

It was early still; Cole's schedule was a few hours off from the rest of the world. Nathan would probably be arriving home from work soon.

Cole grabbed a pair of underwear, his shorts, and the tank top. He sent Nathan a text.

Going to swing by, hope that's okay.

He found his keys and his wallet, yanked on his baseball cap, and headed out the door.

He had no idea what he was doing, no clue if any of this was fair. He just… he needed to see Nathan's face. He needed to ask if they were salvageable. It didn't have to mean right then, right now. Cole could wait. He would. He only needed to *know*, because he couldn't stand being in this indeterminate middle ground a second longer.

In the elevator, he checked his phone, wondering if Nathan had responded. *Nothing, yet. Well, fair enough.* Nathan was probably still at work or just about to leave, which meant, of course, that Cole would beat Nathan home. Annoyed with himself, Cole blew out a sigh. If he was going to hang around in an empty apartment, he should have stayed at his own.

Then again, the grocery store was between his apartment and Nathan's. He could pick up a few things for dinner. That way, even if Nathan was annoyed that Cole had dropped by, Cole would at least have made dinner. And even if Nathan was pissed, Cole could at least assure himself that Nathan had something decent to eat.

He'd make a salad, he decided. It was too hot for anything else.

Chapter Thirty-Seven

"Travis, why don't we talk about this later, okay?" Emily's cheeks were still wet with tears, but when she caught Nathan's eye, her gaze was steady.

"You keep putting this conversation off, babe. It makes me feel like you're putting me off, too. You can see how upsetting that would be, right?"

"I can," Emily said carefully. She had stopped fighting Travis's grip on her arm, and he released her. Nathan refused to let his relief turn into relaxation.

"Thank you." Travis took her hand in his—gently this time. "I'm sorry that I hurt you." He looked at her expectantly.

Nathan's phone was completely free of his pocket, now. He hit the home button. Which side of the touchscreen was the emergency call shortcut on? He tried to picture the lock screen.

"I'm sorry I hurt you too," Emily said.

Travis looked pleased with her apology. Annoyance was rapidly overcoming Nathan's fear. But not quite overcoming, since Nathan's throat was still tight, and he was fully prepared to jump Travis if he reached for Emily again. Nathan didn't expect to stand a chance against Travis, but he figured he'd provide enough distraction that Emily could make it out the door.

The left side. The momentary distraction allowed the image of his lock screen to float to the surface of his consciousness.

Nathan moved his thumb and tapped the spot on the screen he was pretty sure was the emergency call button.

Nothing happened.

Fuck.

The problem with touchscreens, he realized, was that, unless you were looking directly at the screen, there was no way to know if you'd hit the right button, or if you'd hit any button at all. And Nathan had to start hitting buttons fast.

"What's that in your hand?"

Nathan was so focused on his phone and trying to figure out what position the number nine would be on his upside down screen, that he forgot to pay attention to his body language. His elbow stuck out from his side at an awkward angle, one that obviously indicated he had something behind his back.

"What? No. Nothing. Sore. I'm just—I hit my back on the chair." Nathan dropped his phone into his pocket and lifted his empty hands innocently. He wasn't even lying—he had hit his back, and the bruise ached.

"Bullshit," Travis decided. "Give me your phone. You, too," he said to Emily.

"Travis, that seems a little…"

"Give me your phones." Travis held out his hand expectantly.

"Right, it's just that I'm waiting for a text from my—" Nathan started, cutting himself off when Travis' jaw flexed and he took a threatening half-step forward. "Never mind. It'll wait. Here." *God fucking damn it.* Nathan dropped his phone into Travis' outstretched hand. Emily did the same, and they exchanged another quick glance when Travis put both phones in his pocket.

Well. There went Nathan's best and only defense.

Or did it?

Nathan's thoughts jumped up a floor, to the mysterious chest in Jag's bedroom. *There had to be something in the chest that would help, right? A spell. A weapon. A sacrificial dagger, or at the very least a crystal ball he could throw at Travis's stupid handsome head.* If only he'd had a chance to open it, he'd know exactly what to go for!

How was it possible that his afternoon had gone so disastrously wrong? And, for the first time in a long time, his problem was a purely human one. Nathan gritted his teeth. Frustration wouldn't get him or Emily out of the apartment. A cool head and careful thinking might.

"Okay." Travis took a deep breath. Nathan hoped he choked on his spit.

Travis turned to Emily. "Now that we're not going to have any distractions, I'd like to talk about our future."

Heteronormativity: It's a trap! Nathan, now that Travis's attention was elsewhere, rolled his eyes. How was some jealous boyfriend derailing his carefully laid plans even *fair*? Didn't the universe know he had more important things to be doing than this?

Travis gestured at Jag's couch. Emily's hands clenched into fists at her side. Nathan hoped she wasn't going to try to punch Travis—not that he'd blame her for the attempt.

"Sure, Trav." Emily forced a smile and led the way into the living room.

"Hey, um, you know this isn't really my business and I don't want to intrude on such a personal conversation. I'm not trying to leave," he added quickly, in response to Travis's sharp look. "Why don't I just hang out upstairs while you two talk?" *Please work, please work, please work.*

"Thanks, Nathan," Emily said. "That's really thoughtful."

"Isn't it just." Travis eyed Nathan skeptically. "How about we all go upstairs first." It wasn't a question.

"I mean, you guys could go upstairs, and I could stay here," Nathan offered. It was a long shot, but who knew, maybe Travis was as much of a meathead as he looked.

Travis didn't bother to respond to Nathan's offer. He gestured impatiently to the stairs. Emily turned and headed up. Travis waited for Nathan to follow her before he brought up the rear.

The hair on the back of Nathan's neck prickled to have Travis at his back, and the sore spots in his body from when Travis had thrown him into the chair burned with each step Nathan took. He was getting used to this, he thought, to the immediacy of violence.

They reached the second floor, and Emily and Nathan stood to the side of the stairs as Travis stalked through Jag's bedroom. Finding nothing—and Nathan wasn't sure what Travis thought he might find—Travis grunted acquiescence.

"All right. What's your name again?"

"Uh, Nathan," Nathan answered. Was he being held hostage by a guy who didn't even remember his name?

"Nathan. Fine. You can stay here. But I don't want to hear a fucking sound from you—and you don't come down until I say. Understand?"

"Yup." Nathan kept his gaze steady and on Travis. He could see Emily out of the corner of his eye. She also wasn't looking at him but was staring pointedly at the closet.

"Good." Travis dismissed Nathan and held out his hand for Emily. She took it and followed Travis down the stairs.

Once they were out of his line of sight, Nathan let out a slow, quiet breath. He waited, standing by the edge of Jag's bed and jittery with nerves, until he heard Travis and Emily take a seat on Jag's couch. Travis started talking, and Nathan dropped to all fours. The half-wall that kept the second-floor bedroom mostly open to the rest of the loft was the same height and location as Nathan's. He knew from experience that, at a certain angle, a person on the main floor would be able to see someone moving around upstairs. Nathan very much wanted Travis to think that he was sitting patiently on the bed, waiting for his conversation.

For not the first and probably not the last time, Nathan wondered why anyone wanted to date straight men.

On hands and knees Nathan hurried across the carpet to the chest. Kneeling in front of it, he used both hands to push open the heavy lid and peered expectantly inside.

The ancient-looking chest was full of board games. His brain not quite computing, Nathan stared at the boxes. "*The Race to the Midwest, 1846 – 1935*," he mouthed, reading the top of the box closest to him. A picture of a columned building stared out at him. *Chicago's Union Station*, the caption helpfully explained.

Okay. So Jag liked board games. That was fine—so did Nathan. *But Jag had used his love of railway-themed board games to hide his sorcerer shit, right?* Nathan quietly pulled out one box, and then another, and then another, setting them carefully on the carpeted floor of Jag's bedroom. He pulled out thirty-two boxes of railway games, one after another, until the chest sat empty, completely, utterly empty.

Nathan ran his hands along the wooden bottom, the sides, the underside of the curved lid. Each surface was smooth and flat—no apparent secret compartments or hidden drawers. He repeated the inspection, pressing carefully with the tips of his fingers into corners and at the edges of the slats of wood: nothing.

He sat back on his heels, hollowed out and shaken with dismay. He reached for the closest game box, took off the lid, and dumped the contents to the floor. He froze, worried Travis would have heard the pieces thunk to the carpet, but in the living room Travis's monologue didn't miss a beat.

"…don't need to let these other guys manipulate you when I…"

Nathan tuned Travis out and pushed the game pieces around. A board, hex tiles, what appeared to be tiny stock certificates, and train tokens; the smaller pieces were all meticulously arranged in little plastic bags. The gamer in Nathan was impressed.

Nathan grabbed another box and dumped it out. The same. He grabbed a third, a fourth. Game pieces, all of them. Not a single thing item that looked out of place. Just… games and game pieces.

He scrambled away from the empty chest and the unsteady piles of games. *Okay. All right. Jag didn't keep his supernatural stuff in the obvious-looking chest. That was fine. It would be upstairs somewhere, right?*

Nathan crawled to Jag's dresser and began opening drawers.

Chapter Thirty-Eight

COLE TWISTED THE GROCERY BAG between his fingers as he neared Nathan's building. It was a bad idea, heading over unscheduled. He'd been uncomfortable enough with it the first time, and then Nathan had only stopped texting for a few days. This time they'd had a fight—a serious one—and hadn't communicated since. If Nathan was looking for grounds to break up with him…

Well, in that case, Cole supposed the polite thing to do would be to give Nathan an excuse.

He let himself in to the building using his keys and was grateful to be out of the smoke-filled air. Cole's skin still itched, and he had to concentrate to ignore the part of him that insisted he was wasn't safe, that he needed to run, to flee. The scent was muffled inside the building, but he could still taste the acerbic smoke. His head ached, and he fought to close his senses down further.

Deciding the elevator would feel too much like a trap, Cole took the stairs to Nathan's floor. He unlocked Nathan's door without issue, and, kicking off his flip-flops, went into the kitchen with the groceries.

Nathan's kitchen was a mess. Dirty dishes had piled up in the sink, and the recycling bin overflowed with takeout containers. Cole pulled open the cupboard under the sink, and, sure enough, the garbage bin was equally overstuffed.

Considering the sight that had greeted Nathan the last time he'd taken the garbage and recycling down, Cole couldn't blame Nathan for trying to ignore them for as long as possible. He only wished Nathan had said something. Not necessarily to *him*, but Dee or Jamie or Kiara or Ryn. *Or, hell, Isobel, Darren, Cris, Mrs. Ho for goodness' sake. Someone.*

Asking for help wasn't easy. But sometimes it was necessary. Depending on how his conversation with Nathan went today, Cole would raise that point himself—or have a quick chat with Jamie. Nathan was far more apt to accept help from her and Dee than from him if things went south—further south.

Cole unpacked the groceries and put most of them in the nearly empty fridge. He gathered the recycling and the garbage—not just from under the sink, but the bin in Nathan's bedroom and the one from the bathroom—and set them by the front door so he'd remember to take them down.

He noticed Nathan's overflowing laundry bin when he was upstairs and, after a moment's hesitation—*was he making himself too much at home, the way Nathan had made himself too much at home at Cole's?*—put a load of laundry in as well.

He rinsed off the dishes and loaded what fit into the dishwasher. Filling the sink with hot, soapy water, he ignored Nathan's rubber gloves and began to wash the remaining dishes. The water was hot enough that Cole felt the burn against his skin. Usually he found the sensation so unpleasant that he'd wear the gloves—which Nathan hated as he claimed Cole's wider hands stretched them out—but today he appreciated the slight pain. It kept him focused on the task at hand and stopped his brain from running in a million different worried directions about Nathan or the fires from the interior. And it distracted from the pain in his head. All Cole had to focus on was how to remove three-day-old mac and cheese from a pot.

He could do that.

Chapter Thirty-Nine |

NOTHING. NOTHING IN JAG'S BEDROOM indicated any supernatural interest. Jag didn't even read fiction—his bookshelves were full of histories and biographies and textbooks. Nathan couldn't find one single hint of witchcraft or wizardry, not even a deck of Tarot cards!

Nathan ground his fist into the carpet and wished he could punch something instead. He imagined Travis's face, his strong cheekbones and his firm jaw. Nathan imagined how it would feel to plow his fist into Travis's face. It would hurt, but Nathan bet it would be worth it.

He felt, somehow, more helpless against Travis than he had against the Huntsmen. With the Huntsmen, Nathan had been literally outgunned. There was no world in which he could take on a highly-trained militia that specialized in hunting werewolves. *Travis though? Travis was just a guy. A regular guy.*

And so, Nathan was beginning to understand, was Jag. Or he had been, anyway.

But that still didn't make sense. Why was Jag dead? Why the overkill? Why was Jag's bedroom full of normal-person stuff?

Was it possible that Jag kept his sorcery shit downstairs? The kitchen maybe—if potions needed to be brewed or mixed or...

Nathan leaned against Jag's bed in defeat. The carpet was strewn with Jag's belongings: clothes and books and knickknacks. He'd even found Jag's lube and condoms—but not one hint of anything sketchy. Jag didn't even have a bag of weed tucked away upstairs! The only thing in Jag's apartment that was unusual was the abundance of plants.

Was that it? Nathan clung to the new idea with desperate hope. What if it wasn't a spell, but a plant? What was the thought he'd had earlier? *A magic garden.* Maybe the plants worked together, the combination of all these exotic-looking leaves, maybe not even all of them, but some of them—*like* a spell, but different. Plants that, when grown together, when combined somehow…

Nathan's eyes darted around the room, counting, cataloguing the plants. It wouldn't just be a matter of figuring out which specific plants, but there probably had to be an order to destroying them.

He heard Emily's voice, gentle and coaxing, from downstairs:

"Travis, I'd really like to talk about this later. Maybe once we have some privacy…?"

"I told you, we're talking about this now. Now don't interrupt me again, Em. You know I hate that."

Right. Fuck. Different focus. He didn't want to destroy Jag's spells now; Nathan wanted to be able to harness them, to use them to chase off Travis, to get himself and Emily out of the apartment. *Okay,* to do that he'd have to—

Nathan let his head fall back against the mattress and closed his eyes. *Do what? Get a PhD in botany?* What was he thinking, *magic plants? In the apartment of a guy who was in every other way, regular?* Even Nathan, even now, could see insanity in that kind of thought. If he wasted his time upstairs looking for a magic solution to a mundane problem, it wouldn't just be his safety at stake, but Emily's too.

His mouth was dry, his throat was tight, and his eyes burned with tears of angry disappointment. *Was Jag really, truly, just a regular guy?*

What was Nathan's case for Jag-as-supernatural? *Lay it out now,* Nathan told himself. He wished he had his notebook and his spreadsheet.

There'd been that time on the roof, when Jag had appeared out of nowhere. But, Nathan had to concede, it had been dark. And he'd been jittery—with more than a drink or two in him. It was possible he simply hadn't seen Jag, that he'd been too distracted by the suffocating feel of his apartment and his anxiety over being able to sleep.

Then, the body. Jag's body. Blood spilled across the floor like so much red paint. A hideous void where a head should be. The gruesome stumps of his arms. *Too violent to be anything but supernatural*, Nathan had thought. Inhuman violence for a being that *was* inhuman.

The crow next. Furious and screaming. It had followed him in that weird, hopping, forward stalk, as if it had been trying to get him to turn back. *Was it that simple*, Nathan wondered? He'd never witnessed such behavior from a bird. *Just because you didn't,* he reminded himself, *doesn't mean other people haven't.* He'd thought the crow had to be connected with Jag—but maybe the crow had just been a, well, crow, one who didn't want Nathan in its space, for whatever reason. It hadn't attacked him, after all. It hadn't done anything but caw—horribly and terrifyingly—but cawing wasn't exactly uncharacteristic behavior from a crow.

Then the angry cat that scared Arthur and took a swipe at Jamie. Nathan had had a hard time believing that any cat in its right mind would claw at a *werewolf.* It would have to be a cat with a death wish.

Or, really, just a cat.

Hadn't he seen one go after Cris's sweet pit bull Penny, when the pit bull had bounded forward, overly friendly? Penny could have eaten the cat in two large bites, but the cat had puffed up, hissing and spitting, and gone straight for Penny's face with its claws. Penny had beat a hasty retreat, and Cris and Nathan had given the offended feline a wide berth as they'd gone past. It was possible—if not likely, Nathan was forced to admit—that maybe cats were just assholes.

The smoke. A heavy shroud around the city. Not just this city—how many more in the province, in the neighboring provinces, had been affected, Nathan couldn't say. But as much as he'd wanted to believe that the cause had been Jag's death, that Jag had been somehow connected to the elements, it sounded ridiculous. B.C. had forest fires every year. They often sent smoke down the coast. If it was worse this year, if the smoke felt thicker, lingered longer, all that meant was that the fires had been worse. And the explanation for that was tragically simple: climate change as a result of global warming.

And, finally, the two-headed dog. In reality, two whole, separate dogs walking side-by-side on their leashes, a trick of the light and shadows, nothing more. His mind was making shapes, skewed versions of the truth.

Laid out like that, there was no inherent connection between them. Nathan's proof of the supernatural wasn't proof so much as paranoia. Those things had all happened to him, or people close to him, but maybe they were just things that happened and not events triggered by the death of a sorcerer.

Nathan dug his fingers into the carpet and tried to ground himself against the reeling sensation of all his clever threads slipping through his fingers like wet spaghetti. He'd been building a case based on, what? Hope? Anticipation? Desperation?

There was no case, no supernatural mystery surrounding Jag.

The clarity was sudden and stunning, like a blow that hurt too much for pain, a hollow numbness that indicated only that something was wrong, that damage had been done.

Nathan needed to shake himself out of it. He couldn't be numb, not now, not with Travis the dickhead dictator downstairs.

If Jag wasn't supernatural, then his murder wasn't either. It was a regular murder. It was human, despite the gruesomeness, the unnecessary mutilation.

Why though? And who?

"...value what is between us and I don't want that diluted by..."

Nathan lurched upright. *Travis. Fucking of course. The real bad guy, the real monster.* He'd been staring Nathan in the face since he'd run into Travis and Emily in the grocery store. Travis didn't just rub Nathan the wrong way, he gave off murder-y vibes. And Nathan was trapped in an apartment with him.

Chapter Forty |

HOW IS IT, NATHAN WONDERED, *that his year only continued to get worse?*
A laugh threatened to bubble from his chest, and he clamped a hand
over his mouth. He had no time for hysterics. He had a new problem
to solve and fast. *Get out.*

He wouldn't underestimate Travis again. The other man's looming
bulk had seemed an implied threat when he'd stood between Nathan
and Emily and the door. Nathan should have rushed him then; he
shouldn't have waited. He wouldn't make that mistake twice.

So, what was he going to do?

Nathan forced himself to relax against the bed again, to focus his
adrenaline on a solution and not give in to panic. He tried Kiara's
breathing exercises. *In for four. Hold for four. Out for four. In for four.
Hold for four. Out for four.*

All right. He had to accept that he wasn't going to find a magical
wizard staff or charmed dagger or hex bag that would help get him
and Emily out of the situation they'd found themselves in.

Wow. Okay. For the first time in a year Nathan was dealing with
a life and death scenario that was a purely human one. He'd been so
hyper-vigilant about anticipating the next monster that he'd forgotten
the scariest horror movies usually involved human antagonists. Nathan

wasn't sure how he felt. *Relieved?* He had a normal problem that was entirely within his capacity to solve.

Travis wasn't packing super strength and claws, just regular, muscle-y dude-who-works-out strength. And big, meaty fists.

Travis had beheaded a guy—*and what the fuck was that about, Trav?* He probably wasn't above doing it again. Nathan was beginning to put the pieces together, listening with half an ear to Travis's continued speech below.

"...only concerned about your safety..."

Now that he was paying attention, it was easy enough to read between the lines. Travis had killed Jag in the hopes that it would send Emily running into his arms. *Would he do the same to Nathan? To Emily, if she refused?* Nathan knew the stats, that a woman was in the most danger from an intimate partner when she was leaving him.

But Emily wasn't alone, and Nathan decided right there that they were both leaving the apartment intact and as soon as possible. The less time spent with a man who very likely had killed the person whose bedroom Nathan had just destroyed, the better. He'd get them out—whatever it took.

Keeping half of his attention on the conversation downstairs so he'd know the instant something changed, Nathan put his mind on escape plans that did not involve sorcery.

Fourth floor. Narrow front hallway, bathroom off to the right. Kitchen just beyond. Opens into a living space, bank of windows at the end. The bedroom's a small loft up the stairs on the right, over the kitchen. Closets and cupboards only hiding space. One exit; front door. Good soundproofing.

Easy to defend. Hard to escape.

Weapons: nope.

Phone: nope.

Did anyone know his whereabouts: nope.

Okay, so not great. But he had Emily—and that was something.

Hadn't she had tried to tell him something before she'd gone downstairs with Travis? She'd been staring at the closet—pointedly.

Nathan had gone through it as thoroughly as he dared; now he crawled across the floor to it.

His first stroke of luck was that it was in the corner of the room farthest from the stairs, and Nathan felt comfortable rising to a half-crouch. When he'd rooted through it earlier he'd found clothes, a few more board games, some formal wear, nothing particularly sorcerer-y. Nathan rifled through the contents again. A hanger screeched against the metal bar, and Nathan froze, his breath caught in his throat. But Travis's monologue continued uninterrupted.

Nothing. Nothing here would... Nathan spotted it tucked against the back wall. He'd seen it the first time and dismissed it as unimportant. Now that the criteria for his search had moved from magical to practical, however, it took on new significance. He reached past the hanging clothes and pulled out the slender black bag.

He dropped down to the carpet and unzipped it, revealing a paddle neatly stored in three separate pieces: the blade, the middle shaft, and the handle. Nathan slid each piece out. He'd never gone paddle boarding, but suspected that, judging by its size, that was its purpose. Also, Jag only had one paddle. Nathan snapped the pieces together and hefted the finished product in one hand.

Put together, the paddle was well over six feet long. But it was light, real light, which was probably ideal for a paddle boarder and less ideal for Nathan's current situation. Nathan ran a thumb over the edge of the paddle blade.

He and Dee had faced down a murderous werewolf with a stick and an aluminum baseball bat, respectively. He could take *Travis* with a freaking paddle if he had to.

Chapter Forty-One

Cole glanced at the clock on the microwave. It was close to the time Nathan usually got home from work. He had yet to receive a text from Nathan and Cole was having trouble keeping his anxiety in check. *Was Nathan still furious? Or had he simply not had a chance to check his phone? What would his reaction be if he came home and found Cole unannounced in his space?*

Cole wandered out of the kitchen and into the living room. It seemed tidy enough, except for a pile of misshapen bobby pins on the coffee table. *Were they garbage? Some sort of project?* Cole left them as they were. The last thing he wanted to do was disrupt Nathan's life further.

He sank down onto the couch and rested his head in his hands. What was he doing? The last month had been nothing but tottering uncertainty when it came to his relationship with Nathan. They'd taken so long to come together that, when they had, Cole had felt secure, as if the ground under them was firm and the path stretching ahead of them was sturdy. Now everything seemed to crumble at the lightest touch, and Cole didn't know how to reach out to Nathan and bring them both back to solid ground.

He wasn't sure if there was any point in trying. He couldn't carry them both by himself, and, if Nathan didn't want to be with Cole, if

Cole was having to fight Nathan himself *for* Nathan... why bother? Cole didn't want to be with someone who didn't want to be with him. If Nathan would be happier freed of his relationship with Cole, Cole certainly wasn't going to stand in his way.

And what about himself? Cole leaned back, pressing the heels of his hands into his tired eyes. He was so scared of losing Nathan. He'd never felt fear like this. The only thing that came close was when the Huntsmen had taken Nathan. Walking into that absurdly professional boardroom to see Nathan with his glasses broken, a bruise blooming on his cheek, and his lopsided, cocky grin shaky but still in place, Cole had been terrified. In that moment, he would have done anything to get Nathan back. It had frightened him, the extent that Cole had suddenly been willing to consider the possibility of a trade: Ryn for Nathan, a relative stranger for the love of his life. He wasn't sure what he would have done, if Kiara hadn't taken control of the situation and engineered a solution. He didn't like to think about it.

Cole had never been more grateful to cede control to his younger sister.

Now if only she could come up with another clever solution to his current problem.

Cole heaved a sigh and let himself drop sideways onto the couch in an uncommon display of drama. His head pounded. He had no idea how to *be* around Nathan, no idea how to help, no idea how to heal. His instinct was to mother—as evidenced by the tidied apartment. The problem was that each attempt to help Nathan wound up hurting him.

Fuck. Coming over had been a mistake. He should never have shown up without having heard back from Nathan. He *knew* better.

Cole pushed himself upright. He'd go. He'd leave a quick, apologetic note. Nathan was a mess, *he* and Nathan were a mess, and showing up uninvited to tidy a kitchen that wasn't his was not going to fix the underlying problems between them. He went back into the kitchen to find the notepad he'd used last time.

"Hey, are you two done down there, cause I'm getting kinda bored."

Cole stopped, one hand frozen in the drawer, hovering over the pad of paper. A place like an apartment building—dozens of people stacked on top of each other, with dubious soundproofing at best, and humans being so *loud*—was a nightmare cacophony for young werewolves. Once wolves grew into their abilities and learned how to tune out the background noise, the noise was easy to ignore, and, for the most part, Cole didn't register the sound of neighbors going about their daily lives.

Today, especially, Cole was doing everything he could to block out the rest of the world. But the voice that jumped out wasn't one of Nathan's neighbor's, but *Nathan's*.

Chapter Forty-Two

"Hey, are you two done down there, cause I'm getting kinda bored."
Nathan stuck his head over Jag's bedroom's half-wall to peer down at
Travis and Emily in the living room. Emily's eyes flicked up to Nathan,
and then fixed back on Travis; her body was tense as she braced for
whatever happened next.

Good. If Nathan could make Travis come up to him, then Emily
would have a straight shot to the door. Nathan knew, even with his
improvised weapon, that he'd be unlikely to last longer than a few
minutes, but that should be more than enough time for Emily to get
out and call for help.

Travis turned to look up at Nathan; irritation twisted his attractive
face into something ugly. "What did I tell you?"

Nathan shrugged. "Yeah, but, like, c'mon. You can't seriously expect
me to stay up here forever."

Travis's irritation darkened to anger. "I said I don't want to hear
a fucking *sound* from you. Em and I are having a conversation, and
you're interrupting."

"Are you?" Nathan looked doubtful. "It sounds to me, from up
here, where, for the record, I can hear everything—you know this
isn't like, a full wall, right?" He indicated the empty space between
the half-wall and the ceiling. "It sounds like it's more you talking at

Emily than the two of you talking with each other. And if she's even half as bored as I am…" He trailed off with a shrug. "I dunno, man. I don't think things are going your way."

Travis got up from the couch and stormed to the stairs. Nathan backed rapidly away from the half wall. He planted his feet on the carpet and firmed his grip on the paddle, careful to hold it below the lip of the wall so Travis wouldn't see it on his way up.

Travis took the stairs two at a time, and Nathan's palms went slick with sweat. He'd only have one shot at catching Travis off guard, and he'd have to make the most of it.

Travis reached the final step, and Nathan swung the paddle with all his might. It swept up and caught Travis under the chin. Travis teetered on the step. His arms windmilled. Nathan had time to flash a victory grin before Travis's hand caught the rail and he propelled his entire body forward, driving straight for Nathan.

Nathan felt the impact of Travis's shoulder into his stomach, and then they hit the floor and the air was driven from Nathan's lungs for the second time. Nathan strained to recover his breath; the paddle dropped from his nerveless fingers.

Travis rose to straddle Nathan and wrapped his hands around Nathan's throat. He squeezed.

Nathan bucked. Panic surged through his veins; his body was a live wire.

"I think I like using my hands," Travis gritted out between his clenched teeth as he bore down on Nathan's neck.

Nathan clawed at Travis's arms and, when that didn't work, reached for Travis's face. Travis was bigger than Nathan and all brawn, but Nathan was tall and long-limbed. Nathan dug his nails into the side of Travis's face and raked down, leaving bloody furrows. Travis roared in anger and pain, and his grip on Nathan's neck tightened.

Black spiraled at the edges of Nathan's vison. He could feel his arms weaken and his body slow down as his lungs threatened to burst. At least

Emily would be safe. If she had any sense, and Nathan knew she did, she'd have run for the door the second Travis got to the second floor.

Nathan clung to the thought of Emily in the hall and screaming for help as his hands fell like dead weights from Travis's arms.

Chapter Forty-Three

COLE THOUGHT HE WAS HALLUCINATING, and then he heard what was unmistakably Nathan's voice for a second time.

"Yeah, but, like, c'mon. You can't seriously expect me to stay up here forever."

Baffled, Cole cocked his head and listened more intently. Nathan's voice was coming from within the building, but not from where Cole would expect to hear it—the foyer, the parkade, even the gym. It was coming from *above* Nathan's apartment.

A second voice, brutal and blunt-edged with violence, followed Nathan's.

"I said I don't want to hear a fucking *sound* from you."

Cole's body was moving before his brain caught up. He was already outside of Nathan's apartment. The door slammed closed behind him and Cole shoved through the heavy fire door to the stairwell.

He burst onto the fourth floor just as a woman flew out of one of the apartments.

"Help! Oh, my god, he's going to kill him." Her wide, wild eyes fixed on Cole. The scent of her fear was tart and thick on Cole's tongue. "Call 911!"

"I am 911," Cole informed her. He yanked his phone out of his pocket and thrust it into her hands as he raced past her. "But call anyway."

He made it up the stairs in time to see Nathan's hands fall limply away from the man on top of him.

Fury raged through Cole, and he felt the sudden sharpness of fangs in his mouth even as his eyes flashed from honey-brown to winter-gray. When Cole moved, there was no disconnect between his intentions and his actions. His hand closed around the stranger's shoulder. Nails harder and sharper than a human's had any right to be sliced through the fabric of the man's shirt and into his skin.

The man yelped. His hands lifted from Nathan's throat. Nathan coughed, a horrible, choking sound, and desperately sucked in a mouthful of air.

He was not dead yet. The hurricane of Cole's fury unleashed, and he lifted the man up and off—and flung him down the stairs. Travis hit the wall on his way down and crumpled to the floor.

Cole was at Nathan's side in an instant. "Don't move," he ordered. Claws melted back to fingers. He began a careful examination of Nathan's body, checking for other injuries. Nathan disregarded Cole's instructions and clutched a fistful of Cole's shorts; water streamed from his eyes as he heaved in breath after breath.

"You're okay; I've got you," Cole promised. Nathan closed his eyes and nodded weakly. Cole cupped Nathan's cheek in his hand and lowered his forehead to Nathan's. The adrenaline that had flooded his body was fading, and terror swooped in in its wake. He'd heard the way Nathan's pulse had slowed, a thunderous stampede to settling dust as Cole had flown up the stairs. Nathan had been seconds away from losing consciousness, and, if that had happened, the damage might have been irreversible. As it stood, Nathan had a collar of bruises blooming at his neck.

What would have happened, Cole wondered, if he hadn't been fast enough? He wasn't sure if he would have been able to stop himself.

If whoever the hell it was who'd been on top of Nathan had killed him—Cole didn't think he'd have waited for an explanation, or for the human justice system to do its job. He'd have killed the man he'd just thrown down the stairs.

The man groaned, and Cole could hear him begin to stir. *Good.* He'd be conscious enough to talk to the authorities. The wail of sirens closed in, and Cole curled himself closer around Nathan.

Chapter Forty-Four

NATHAN SAT IN THE BACK of an ambulance with a blanket around his shoulders as lights flashed silently over the street. It was exactly like the scene at the end of a horror movie, where the survivors were handed cups of coffee and consoling words. Nathan didn't have coffee, but someone had pressed a bottle of water into his hands. His throat *hurt*. His head hurt. His back hurt; his butt hurt; his stomach hurt. His exhaustion went way beyond the physical.

Cole stood a few feet away, listening intently to another paramedic. He looked at Nathan every minute or so, and each time Nathan rolled his eyes and lifted his hand to wave so that Cole would know he was still alive.

"Well, that sucked." Emily hopped up beside Nathan. She had a blanket as well and toyed with the edges of it. Considering the heat, the blankets were ridiculous, but part of his core wouldn't warm.

"Yeah. Really did." Nathan's voice was a barely audible rasp.

They sat in silence. "He'd been bugging me, Travis. He gave me a set of keys to his place a few months ago. Turns out the keychain wasn't just a keychain."

Shit. Nathan untucked his arm from the blanket, lifted it around Emily's shoulders, and pulled her to his side. She bent forward.

"He heard me and Jag. He heard everything. Everything I've been doing. Everyone I've spoken to. Anywhere I had my keys, my purse. He could listen. Is it my fault for not seeing this?" Emily asked in a whisper, barely audible over the ambient noise of the emergency services. "For not seeing the potential of this in him?" She gestured with her head to where Travis sat in the back of a cop car. After the paramedics had looked him over and determined that he'd only suffered bruises and scrapes, Nathan had watched him be handcuffed. It had been great.

"No," Nathan said honestly and hoarsely. "We see what we want to see, sometimes."

"He killed Jag, I guess." Emily balled her hand into a fist around the blanket. "Because Jag touched me, because he kissed me. I kissed him back," she said defiantly. "I touched him back. Well—" she broke into a laugh that ended sounding suspiciously like a sob. "I grabbed his butt."

Nathan's shoulder shook with laughter that hurt too much to vocalize. "He had a good butt," he agreed, thinking of the few times he'd seen Jag around the building.

"He did," Emily said sadly. "I think, I think I loved him too, a little. He never got to know that, though. I never told him. And now, because of Travis, I'll never be able to."

"I'm sorry." Nathan leaned his cheek against the top of her head and gave as much comfort as he could.

"And I loved Travis. Not now, and I don't think I have for a while, but I did love him." Emily pulled away so that she could look Nathan in the eyes. "I loved him," she repeated.

"It's okay." Nathan grabbed her hand and squeezed. "You saw the best in him. The good parts. That was real. What you felt was real. You just…" He groped for the right words. "You didn't have all the information."

"What if I did and I just ignored it?"

Nathan shook his head. "You didn't see it because he didn't want you to see it. This isn't your fault."

"Promise?"

"Promise."

Emily gave a loud sniff and brushed discreetly at her cheeks. "Your boyfriend's coming over. You know," she added. "He can run really fast."

Nathan nodded. "Yeah, he can."

Cole had indeed broken away from his conversation and walked up to them. "How are you feeling?" he asked them.

"I'm fine." Emily kissed Nathan's cheek before hopping off the truck. "I think I have to go to the station, give a statement or something." She looked at Detective Mira emerging from the building.

"I'm okay." Nathan wanted to stop talking for perhaps the first time in his life.

"We're taking you to get tested," Cole informed Nathan. "I want to get some X-rays: soft tissue neck and cervical spine."

"What about...?" Nathan jerked his chin in the direction of the cops.

Cole shook his head. "I spoke to them. We'll go in later this week, once you've had a chance to recover." He paused and when he spoke again his expression had changed from personal to professional. "You, I mean. You'll go in. I can go with you, obviously, if you want. But I can also... not. If that's what you want."

Nathan glanced around to make sure that no one else was within earshot. "You were right," he said. "About Jag. He wasn't anything..." Special, Nathan had been about to say *anything special*, but that wasn't true, was it? Jag had been a friend, an almost-lover, a son, an enthusiast of both paddle boards and board games. And plants. He'd liked sweater vests and biographies about famous scientists. He'd loved Emily. "He wasn't what I thought he was," Nathan finished.

It was too much to deal with, right now, the knowledge that he'd been wrong about Jag, that he'd seen what he wanted to see, and not what was actually there. Nathan was dog-tired and hurting and all he wanted in the entire world was to fall asleep with Cole's arms wrapped tight around him.

Cole didn't say anything in response to Nathan's admission. Nathan figured he couldn't blame Cole—not when every other conversation they'd had about Jag had resulted in a fight. Nathan's heart joined the various other body parts that hurt. He wasn't sure what he believed anymore. If Jag was a regular human, did that mean that Cole and the other werewolves were right, that it was just them? Or had Nathan jumped too quickly to a conclusion—was his initial theory right, just not about Jag? Even beginning to think about it again was exhausting.

"I want you to come with me." Nathan looked up at Cole. "To the hospital, for whatever tests. To the police station later. To bed." He gave a lopsided smile at the look on Cole's face. "I want you with me." He freed his arm from the blanket and held out his hand. Cole took it; his grip was firm and warm and steady.

"All right," Cole agreed. His throat worked, and Nathan leaned forward to rest his head against the sturdy planes of Cole's chest. Cole brought his arm around Nathan and held him close.

Chapter Forty-Five |

Cole rode in the back of the ambulance with him. Uncomfortable enough already with the amount of attention he'd received—from the police to the paramedics—Nathan was glad it was just the two of them. He gave Cole's hand a squeeze.

Cole squeezed back. "You're gonna be okay," he promised. "I'll make sure of it."

"I 'm not worried." Nathan murmured. He wasn't sure how he felt, but concern for his physical well-being wasn't high on his list. His throat and neck *hurt*. Every time he swallowed it was like drinking razor blades. But it was nothing dire. He'd recover. He'd heal.

The rest of him though… Nathan wasn't sure. He wasn't sure of anything, anymore. He'd been certain, so certain that Jag had been like Jamie, like Cole.

He'd been wrong.

All his research, his notes—he'd spent a month trying to prove something that wasn't real. *Jesus.* Nathan closed his eyes from where he lay on the stretcher Cole had insisted he stay on.

He'd met with the Huntress, set up a meeting behind everyone's backs. Nothing had come of it, but he was going to have to tell everyone. He couldn't keep it a secret, not anymore.

"Hey, it's over." Cole reached down; his thumb was gentle as he wiped away the tear that had slid down Nathan's cheek. "You're safe. Emily is safe. Travis was arrested. He won't come for you." Now Cole's voice turned fierce; the low growl of wolf rumbled just beneath the surface. "I won't let him."

Nathan nodded and leaned into the touch of Cole's hand on his face. Cole had had it the wrong way round when he'd worried that Nathan wouldn't want him. What if, when Cole found out everything, he wouldn't want Nathan?

The thought was too much for Nathan to bear. He kept his eyes closed and gripped Cole's hand. For now, at least, he had him.

EVERYTHING MOVED QUICKLY ONCE THEY arrived at the hospital. Cole seemed to know everyone, from the nurses in the emergency room to the X-ray tech. Nathan wasn't sure, but suspected that he was being treated with undo care and speed. Guilt returned, and he found himself grateful that his injuries meant he wasn't supposed to do much speaking.

It was easier to smile and nod. Cole's hand was in his, or on his shoulder, or rubbing at his beard as he spoke to someone in scrubs. Cole was liked and respected. People wanted to help Nathan because they wanted to help Cole.

What had Nathan done to help Cole? Pushed him away. Lied to him. Nathan had accused Cole of keeping secrets, but Nathan had been the one acting on his own.

If he'd left it alone, if he'd never started down his *what if* rabbit hole, none of this would have happened. If he'd trusted Cole, and Kiara, and Jamie, and Dee. God, Dee.

Nathan's shoulders slumped in the wheelchair while he waited for the X-rays. When the truth came out, how many friends would he have left?

Ryn, maybe. The thought brought a rueful smile to Nathan's face. If anyone could appreciate Nathan acting on his own, it was them.

But he had reached out to the Huntsmen, who'd spent a good chunk of February trying to capture or kill Ryn. So maybe he'd lay fifty-fifty odds on Ryn having his back.

That was still better odds than the rest of the pack.

Cole returned and crouched at Nathan's side with his hand reassuringly on Nathan's knee. "They're going to take you in now. It shouldn't be too long. I'll be in the waiting room, and if the x-rays are clear we can go home. Okay?"

Nathan nodded. Cole's eyes had gone back to whiskey-gold. Nathan had seen them flash, wolf-gray and wild, when he'd pulled Travis off Nathan. Now all that wild fury was gone, replaced with reassuring warmth.

Cole pressed a long kiss to Nathan's temple before he rose and let the nurse take Nathan in. Nathan balled his hands into fists in his lap and tried not to think about what would happen when he came clean.

THE X-RAYS WERE OVER FASTER than he expected, and he was wheeled back to the waiting room after less than an hour. Nathan braced himself as the nurse turned the corner and the waiting room came into view.

He'd expected Cole, who was leaning forward with his elbows on his knees in a chair. Nathan hadn't expected to see Jamie flipping through a waiting room magazine beside him or Kiara pacing under the muted television. Ryn sprawled over a chair on the other side of the room, with their long legs splayed out carelessly so their black combat boots created a tripping hazard.

Nathan's heart clenched in his chest; he was overwhelmed.

"Nathan!" Dee's shrieked as she barreled down the hallway. Nathan grinned, so wide it felt like his face might split, and pushed himself out of the chair to meet her. She threw herself at him so hard that Nathan stumbled back, not prepared for their combined weight. Jamie moved fast—faster than Dee—and steadied them both with a hand on his back as Dee wrapped her arms around him.

He wrapped back and buried his face into her hair. They stayed like that until Nathan could feel Dee's tears soak through the fabric of his shirt, and finally she eased back.

"I knew if I went to the bathroom you'd come out the second I was gone," she said with a sniff and punched him lightly on the arm. Her gaze fell to the ring of bruises around his neck, and her green eyes welled again with fresh tears.

"Hey, hey, I'm okay." Nathan pulled her in. Cole met his eyes over Deanna's head, and Nathan mouthed "thank you."

Jamie hugged him next. He inhaled the comforting scent of her cologne, and his own eyes began to sting.

Kiara waited until Jamie let him go, then gave him a quick, fierce hug of her own. "Next time," she growled in his ear, "Call me!"

Nathan rolled his eyes and pushed her playfully back. Ryn eased themselves up from their chair and sauntered across the room. They clapped Nathan on the back and, when their eyes met, Ryn winked. "I hear you played hero. Again."

Uncomfortable with the praise, Nathan shifted his weight. "Moron, more like. Trust me, if I'd known I was going to be choked out, I would have done things a bit differently," he rasped. It was the most he'd said since they'd arrived at the hospital, and he dropped his gaze to avoid the sympathetic looks of his friends.

Cole shouldered his way to Nathan's side. "We've got plenty of time to talk about this later."

That's what Nathan was worried about.

"For now, let's get you home." Cole looked expectantly at the doctor who came through the door of the waiting room. She kept her hands tucked into the pockets of her white coat as she waited for the reunion to finish.

"He's good to go," Dr. Norgard confirmed. "You'll need to keep an eye on him." She spoke directly to Nathan. "If you experience any vomiting, fainting, or persistent headaches, come back in. However, most victims of strangulation—"

Deanna made a muffled noise of dismay.

"—fully recover with no further symptoms. It's going to be a rough few days speaking and swallowing, but as long as you take it easy and get plenty of rest, I don't anticipate further problems." She gave him a reassuring smile, and Cole went to shake her hand and thank her.

Dee found Nathan's hand and held it tight. Ryn grabbed the wheelchair and jerked their chin at Nathan. "Hop in."

Nathan looked askance. "Walk," he insisted.

Ryn smirked and looked expectantly at Cole as he returned.

"Sorry, Nathan." Cole squeezed Nathan's shoulder. "It's hospital policy."

Nathan sighed and sat down. Ryn wheeled him out, as Kiara went ahead to grab the car.

"I'll come over, obviously." Dee kept Nathan's hand in his as they made their way through the hospital. "We'll get takeout from that place with the soup you like. I know they don't do delivery…" She anticipated Nathan's argument. "…but I can use Skip the Dishes. We can hang out, watch a movie. Or you can go straight to bed." She nodded, apparently to herself. "Yeah. We'll get takeout after, once you're awake again. Do you want to eat? Should you eat first? Will that help you sleep? I—"

"Dee," Nathan croaked. "Not tonight, okay?" He knew she only wanted to help, and the last thing Nathan wanted to do was to hurt her feelings. But he needed rest—already he could feel the events of the day and his lack of sleep catching up with him. Dee was a lot of fantastic things, but one of the things she was not was restful.

Deanna sighed and gave his hand another squeeze. "Yeah, okay," she conceded. "I know." She looked down, caught his eye, and rolled her own ruefully. "I know you just want to cuddle with your boyfriend and go to bed. I'm not offended." She kissed his knuckles. "I'm really, really glad you're okay." Her eyes welled up, and Jamie handed her a tissue as tears spilled down her cheeks.

It was Nathan's turn to plant a kiss on her knuckles.

Ryn wheeled him out of the hospital to where Kiara was waiting with the car. Nathan stood and hugged Jamie again, then Dee, holding on long enough that Kiara tapped impatiently on the car's horn.

They broke apart. Cole took the wheelchair inside, and Deanna gave Nathan another quick hug.

"I'll call Darren and Isobel and let them know you're fine. I texted them when we were on our way to the hospital. I figured you'd want them to know, but wouldn't want to have to tell them yourself." Deanna grinned.

She wasn't his best friend for nothing.

"Thank you," Nathan said, relieved that he wouldn't have to try to figure out what to tell them and how. Dee would make sure that they got the non-werewolf version of events. He could wait until tomorrow to contact them.

"Get in!" Kiara yelled from the car's open window. "I'm not supposed to stop here."

"We're coming!" Ryn hollered back. Nathan waved as Dee and Jamie headed to find their car and let Cole help him into the back seat.

Kiara twisted around in her seat as Nathan buckled up. "Your place?" she asked.

Nathan hesitated, then shook his head. "No. Yours." He glanced at Cole, hoping that was all right. After what had happened… Nathan wasn't sure he'd be able to walk into his building without picturing Jag's body and without nightmares of being trapped.

"Ours it is." Kiara agreed and started the car.

"I'm glad." Cole spoke low, though of course, being werewolves, both Kiara and Ryn would have no trouble hearing from the front seat. "I miss having you in my bed."

"No beejays, okay?" Ryn tilted their head back. "My guy needs to rest his throat."

Cole flushed a bright red, and Nathan wheezed with silent laughter.

"That's not what I meant," Cole muttered.

Nathan found Cole's hand and twined their fingers together as the city rolled past.

Chapter Forty-Six

KIARA DROPPED COLE AND NATHAN off at the apartment. She and Ryn had plans for the evening—and now that Nathan wasn't in immediate medical danger, she'd like to return to those plans, she'd informed them. Cole lifted a hand in thanks as the car pulled away, and Ryn waved back at him.

Cole turned to Nathan, feeling suddenly awkward. Nathan's face was pale behind his glasses; his eyes were bruised and bloodshot. How much was from insomnia, and how much from the attack, Cole wasn't sure. His long throat was swollen. It was marked red, blue, and a purple nearly black in places. Now that they were safe, that the man who'd attacked Nathan was behind bars, Cole's fury returned with a vengeance.

"Let's get you inside," he said brusquely. He opened the door with his fob and ushered Nathan in. Anger coiled in his chest like an animal waiting to be unleashed.

Nathan followed Cole to the elevator, and his uncharacteristic silence—something else Cole had to thank Travis for—fed Cole's rage. As they rode up to Cole's floor, Cole wished he hadn't been so lenient with Travis. Once he'd established that Nathan had been okay, that he was out of any immediate danger, Cole should have gone down those stairs and finished the job, made certain that Travis couldn't hurt Nathan the way he'd hurt Jag.

"You 'kay?" Nathan's voice rasped behind him as Cole unlocked the door of the apartment.

"Yes." Cole dropped his keys on the side table with a clatter. "No," he amended, rubbing a rough hand over his face. "No."

"Hey." Nathan reached out and cupped Cole's face in his hands. Cole closed his eyes and allowed Nathan to press their foreheads together.

"It's over," Nathan said. "All of it. I'm done."

Cole jerked back, alarm like a bucket of ice water down his back. "Nathan—"

"No, jeeze." Nathan shook his head, lips quirked in amusement. "The supernatural stuff. I was wrong about Jag."

Cole shook his own head. "That doesn't matter," he said gruffly. If Nathan wanted to spend the rest of his life searching for phoenixes, or gargoyles, or were-tortoises, Cole'd be there to help.

"It matters," Nathan retorted in his whisper-rasp of a voice. "I'm sorry."

Not trusting his own voice, Cole swallowed past the lump in his throat.

"Now please tell me," Nathan continued, "why you're barefoot."

Cole and Nathan looked down simultaneously at Cole's feet, which were indeed bare.

"Oh." Cole winced. "I was, uh, in your apartment."

Nathan blinked in surprise.

"That's how I got there so fast," Cole explained. "I heard your voice."

Nathan went quiet. Cole followed him farther into the apartment and took the chair when Nathan sank onto the couch. "You were checking up on me," he said, finally.

Cole opened his mouth to deny it and stopped. "Yes," he admitted. "I was."

Nathan cracked a wry grin. "Too bad you weren't a couple hours earlier. We could have avoided all this." He gestured at his neck.

Cole rose from the chair and crossed the room to kneel at Nathan's feet. "Whatever you need," he swore. "Whatever it takes. Whatever space, or time, or distance. Whatever you need," he repeated. "I'm here. Just tell me. Please don't shut me out again." He couldn't take that a second time. He wasn't sure where this left him and Nathan, whether the truth about Jag would be the nail in their coffin, but he knew that he'd be there for Nathan however he could.

Nathan stroked Cole's hair. "I thought *I* was the dramatic one."

"Stop joking," Cole scolded. "You aren't supposed to be talking."

"I love you," Nathan said directly into Cole's eyes; his own were wide and blue and earnest.

Relief flowed through Cole like a sigh and he swayed forward with the force of it. "Yeah. Yeah."

"*Yeah?*"

"Yeah. No. I mean—yes. I love you, too. I don't think I can't not. Ever. So, yeah," he said, confidence growing. "Yeah."

"Now it's too much drama. C'mere." Nathan held his arms out, and Cole came into them.

He lay there, his cheek against the strong beat of Nathan's heart. He'd almost been too late. Nathan's neck was proof of that. If he hadn't been so locked down against the smoke, if he'd been thinking less about himself and more about his mess of a boyfriend—

He drew in a shuddering breath. There was no sense in blaming himself for what had already happened and was now out of his control. It was better to focus on what had gone right: that he *had* heard Nathan, that he had shown up in time to save Nathan's life. In the end, Nathan's heartbeat steady against his ear was the only thing that mattered.

He took another deep breath. "You... stink."

Nathan groaned.

"C'mon, let's get you in the shower." Cole stood and held out a hand for Nathan.

Nathan sighed and, with a decidedly unimpressed look, allowed Cole to help him to his feet.

Chapter Forty-Seven |

NATHAN LET COLE LEAD HIM into the bathroom. It had been a few days since he'd found time to shower, so he couldn't blame Cole. Plus, Cole's shower was way nicer than his.

Cole took Nathan's glasses and helped Nathan out of his shirt. He knelt to work off his socks and jeans. Nathan didn't need the help, not exactly. But Cole needed to give it. And Nathan… maybe Nathan needed to receive it.

Cole started the shower and adjusted the heat until steam began to billow out. Nathan liked it hot, liked to stand until he was beet-red and glowing. Cole stepped aside to let Nathan pass and pulled off his own shirt as Nathan tipped his head back under the spray.

The lighting in the shower was too bright to be romantic. Nathan blinked his eyes open when Cole stepped into the shower with him. Cole's muscular body looked tired, and his shoulders were weary, but, when his gaze met Nathan's, his eyes were warm and alive.

Nathan closed his eyes again and let his head fall under the spray. He felt Cole move closer, felt the brush of his arm against Nathan's as he reached around him for the soap.

They were nearly chest to chest. Nathan left his arms at his sides. He let Cole run the pine-scented lather down his skin. His hands smooth and gentle, a soothing contrast to Travis's cruel brutality.

Cole started at the base of Nathan's neck and worked his way down, avoiding the collar of bruises. Though he tried not to be, Nathan remained tense until Cole's fingers drifted down the curve of his shoulders.

Cole smoothed his hands down Nathan's left bicep, paused to get more soap, then continued down Nathan's forearm to his hand. He soaped Nathan's fingers between his, pulling lightly on the joints until Nathan's arm went liquid. Cole repeated his gentle motions on Nathan's right arm, turning him into the spray this way and that to wash the soap from both arms before he focused his attention on Nathan's front.

Travis's initial blow hadn't left a visible bruise, but Nathan flinched when Cole's soapy fingers glided over the tender flesh. Cole murmured a wordless noise of pity that Nathan could barely hear over the cascade of water and gentled his hands further. His palms slid down Nathan's stomach and smoothed up his sides. Cole lifted Nathan's arm and soaped underneath; his fingers carded lightly through the hair at Nathan's armpits. Nathan shivered; neither of them was in the mood for arousal, but it tingled pleasantly nevertheless down his spine.

Nathan kept his eyes closed as Cole guided him back to the spray, trusting easily in Cole's broad hand against his back. He bowed his head forward, breathing in a lungful of moist, steamy, pine-scented air. Water ran behind his ears and down the side of his face, streaming off his nose and down.

Cole's hands were across his shoulders again. Nathan forgot to tense when they drifted across the base of his neck. He had not registered their presence as anything remarkable until they'd passed. Cole trailed soapy fingers down Nathan's spine, then over and across the slight flare of his ass.

Cole knelt, as he had knelt at Nathan's feet, and continued his gentle, thorough wash. He worked his hand between Nathan's cheeks, then down the firm muscle of Nathan's thigh to his feet, repeating on Nathan's other side.

Nathan's body was so lax that he felt like putty in Cole's hands, like something malleable held together only by moisture and heat. Cole pressed on Nathan's hips to move him, and Nathan obeyed.

His eyes stayed closed when Cole drew lather across his groin. Cole's hand was soft on Nathan's cock and balls before he moved down Nathan's thighs. Nathan couldn't remember the last time he'd felt like this. Not just bone-tired, but tranquil. For once, he wasn't worried about sleeping.

When Cole stood, he opened his eyes and blinked water out of them. Cole leaned forward, and his soft lips brushed over Nathan's. Cole pulled back as his soapy hands came to Nathan's shoulders.

"Okay?" he asked.

Nathan sucked on his bottom lip. "Yeah," he croaked.

Cole smiled, his gold eyes crinkling at the corners, and brought one hand up the side of Nathan's neck.

Nathan held Cole's gaze with his. He refused to let Travis take this from him and he held fast to Cole's steady, reassuring gaze.

Cole's fingers were feather-light over the damaged skin, so that Nathan barely registered their presence. He let out a breath he hadn't realized he was holding when Cole lowered his hand.

"I'm going to do the other side next," Cole told him. Nathan nodded, and only then understood that Cole hadn't wanted to place both of his hands around Nathan's neck at the same time. Nathan forced himself to breathe, to let Cole touch his neck and not let it paralyze him.

After that, Cole traded his body soap for the fancy face stuff that Nathan liked and Cole had taken to keeping on hand. Cole worked the soap into a lather. With a light touch on Nathan's chin, he tilted Nathan's head back and then began to massage the pads of his fingers over Nathan's forehead. He worked down the bridge of Nathan's nose, over his cheekbones, down across his jaw. Nathan surrendered entirely to Cole's touch and allowed himself to be turned to face the spray as Cole's hands smoothed any last traces of the soap from him.

Nathan's hair was last, and he swayed toward the touch of Cole's strong fingers as they worked shampoo into his scalp. He felt languid. The heat and Cole's touch worked away any last ounce of stress in Nathan's body until he was certain his bones had turned to Jell-O.

"Good?" Cole asked, once he'd rinsed Nathan's hair.

Nathan nodded, unwilling to break the silence. Not because it hurt to speak—though it did—but because Cole was taking care of him and Nathan was letting him. They didn't need any more words, not now.

Cole shut off the water and pulled a fluffy gray towel off the rack. He wrapped it around Nathan's shoulders before grabbing one for himself.

Nathan fought to stay awake while Cole toweled them off. He took the glass of water Cole pressed into his hand, and obediently swallowed the two small white pills Cole passed him.

"Finish the glass," Cole told him.

Nathan sighed, knowing the pain would slice like razors. But Cole was right, he couldn't afford to be dehydrated. Nathan drank the rest of the water with a grimace, and returned the empty glass to Cole, who traded it for the pair of pajama bottoms that Nathan kept in Cole's top drawer.

Nathan pulled the pants over his hips, and Cole refilled the glass before he led them into the bedroom. Nathan moaned and regretted it when the pain flared. *Whatever. It was worth it.* He couldn't remember the last time he'd been so grateful to see a bed.

Cole had pulled the blackout blinds down over the windows to block the late evening sun. It was hard to believe that only a handful of hours had passed since Nathan had attempted to break the lock on Jag's front door. The bedside lamps were lit, and in their warm glow Nathan crawled across the bed to his usual side.

Cole put the glass of water down beside Nathan and tucked the blankets around him before he settled in on his side of the bed. He turned off the lights and curled his body around Nathan; the heat of his naked body tingled against Nathan's skin.

Nathan snuggled into Cole and pulled his arm around his chest. Cole's breathing was rhythmic and soothing against his back, and Cole's breath was soft on the bare skin of Nathan's shoulder.

Nathan closed his eyes and slept.

HE WOKE UP DISORIENTED. IT was dark, and he didn't know what time it was. Cole's weight had shifted; one leg was thrown across Nathan's since he'd twisted his upper half nearly onto his stomach. Nathan had no idea how the position could be comfortable, but Cole was dead asleep.

Something had woken him. Nathan frowned. Usually when he woke up abruptly, it was from a nightmare. But no cold sweat covered Nathan's skin, nor was a lingering copper taste of terror in his mouth.

He heard a soft thud from outside the bedroom, then a muffled "*Fuck!*"

Nathan breathed out a laugh. Just Kiara, home from her date.

Nathan dropped back to the mattress and wriggled closer to Cole; a vast feeling of contentment rose inside him. Cole murmured, brought Nathan closer, and nuzzled into the soft curls of Nathan's hair.

A stool scraped across the floor in the kitchen, and the freezer door opened and closed as Kiara treated herself to her customary post-date ice cream. Nathan closed his eyes and knew he was safe.

Chapter Forty-Eight |

THE SMOKE HAD FINALLY LIFTED, and the mountains were no longer hidden by the haze. Blue sky was a sudden breath of fresh air, and Cole wasted no time in getting Nathan out in it.

Too much time in Cole's apartment and the place would start to seem like Nathan's sickbed—something which was not helped by the six potted orchids Mrs. Ho had had delivered yesterday.

How she got Cole's address he wasn't sure and figured it was best not to ask.

It wasn't that Cole didn't appreciate the flowers, but nature was so much better if a person could be immersed in it. He took another lungful of the summer air, rich with the scent of sun-warmed earth and growing things, edged with the salt of the ocean.

Nathan groaned and made a face at Cole from behind his sunglasses. "Can't we go back in?"

"No," Cole said cheerfully, taking Nathan's hand in his as they strolled down the seawall. "It's a beautiful day, and it's good for you to get outside and get some exercise."

"Hey," Nathan huffed. "It's hardly like I'm out of shape."

"You're healing, and this will help. If you make it to Granville Island, I'll buy you a cold-pressed juice. Any flavor you want."

"Oh, joy." Nathan's sarcasm was thick enough to chew. And that was ironic, as he still wasn't up to solid foods.

His voice had improved, for which Cole was grateful. For a few days after Travis's attack, Nathan had been silent save for the occasional, rasping whisper. Cole had missed Nathan's complaining and couldn't help being pleased that it was back, albeit somewhat huskier than usual.

The bruises remained awful and vivid. The second day, Dee had dropped by with an armful of scarves and spent an hour teaching Nathan how to tie each one.

As if Nathan could follow the direction of Cole's thoughts, he tugged irritably at the elegant silk scarf around his neck. Between the scarf, his high-collared dress shirt, and the sunglasses, Nathan looked like a movie star. The sad moue on his face completed the image.

"Give it a few minutes." Cole relented. "If you still hate it, we can go back in."

"No," Nathan said grudgingly. "It's fine. I'll live." He heaved a sigh, but his fingers curled closer around Cole's.

They walked in comfortable silence.

"I'm sorry I shut you out," Nathan said suddenly. "I didn't... It's too much, sometimes. Or, it's not too much, you're not too much," he clarified. "But I'm not going to be a person whose first instinct is to share everything."

Cole looked out over the water at the forest of sailboat masts anchored in tidy rows. His jaw tightened. "I'm not asking you to share everything. I'm asking you to communicate, to tell me if you need a few days. I'm always happy to respect that. If you want space, that's never a problem."

"I know." Nathan swallowed. "It's nothing you're doing, or not doing. It's not you, it's me. Look." He stopped, grabbed both of Cole's hands in his, and forced Cole's gaze to meet his through their sunglasses. "I love that you love me. I love how you love me. I love that you want to know how I'm doing, that you care about the state of my apartment, and that you have spent the last four days force-feeding me a liquid diet." He took a deep breath. "Sometimes, though, that's going to make me feel trapped."

Cole's arms gave an abortive jerk as he fought his instinct to yank his hands free of Nathan's. "You're not giving me much to go on here," he said gruffly. "I can't change. I can't care about you any less. If that won't—"

"No," Nathan interrupted. "Let me finish."

Cole pressed his lips together and made himself trust in the solidity of Nathan's hands against his.

"I don't want you to change. I love you. I love watching you fuss like a mother hen. I love your big, soft heart and your big, soft belly. I want to spend the next sixty years of my life coming home to you. And that is where you're going to have to trust me. Because I'm going to be better about telling you when I need space, and so I need you to trust that I'll come back. That every time I get freaked, that I panic, that the walls start to close in, and so I run—I'll come back. If you can let me go, I promise you, I'll come back. I'll come home."

Oh.

Cole closed his eyes, mute with the swell of emotion that overcame him. He'd never gone so far as to ask Nathan for a future; he'd not been sure he'd like the answer. And here it was, offered.

"Then I'll be there." Cole opened his eyes and closed the slight distance between them. He drew Nathan's face down to his. The kiss was soft and slow—an easy merging of two parts.

AT THE MARKET, COLE BOUGHT Nathan a cup of cold pressed blackcurrant and apple juice and chose orange for himself. Nathan finished his in a matter of minutes, and as they headed back down the seawall towards home, helped himself to the rest of Cole's.

The sun glittered on the water, and above them gulls wheeled and called in the cloudless sky.

Chapter Forty-Nine |

DEE PASSED NATHAN A GLASS, and he wrapped it in packing paper before tucking it into a box. It had been two weeks since Nathan had last been in Jag's apartment. He wasn't sure how he'd feel, going back, but Emily had answered the door—a familiar gold bangle bright around her wrist—and pulled him into a tight hug. There'd been music and people Nathan didn't know scattered throughout the space. Nathan had introduced Deanna to Emily, and they'd been swept up in the packing party before Nathan could think twice.

For an accountant, Jag had had some fun friends and family. Nathan and Dee had met at Nathan's apartment ahead of time to discuss strategy for what they'd anticipated would be a somber event.

As though she could read his mind, Dee grinned when she handed him the next glass. "I definitely didn't expect the dancing."

"Me neither." Nathan glanced over his shoulder to where Jag's mom and another of his friends were shaking their butts to the desert blues band that had been one of Jag's favorites. Nathan hoped that people would dance at his funeral, or apartment-pack-up party—ideally both.

In the two weeks since Nathan's encounter with Travis, this was the first time he'd had more than a few minutes alone with Dee. It wasn't on purpose, Nathan was sure, but their large, intrusive friend group—a pack, if you will—made one-on-one time hard. Add in the week Nathan took off work to recover, which he spent mostly sleeping, and Dee's increased responsibility at work… There simply hadn't been time for them to spend time alone.

And maybe Nathan had been avoiding it a little.

They'd seen each other at the hospital. Afterward, someone else was always around, and since they'd been pretending everything was fine they couldn't suddenly stop talking to each other again, not that Nathan thought that was likely to happen. But the worry that it might had kept him from reaching out to make a Dee-and-Nathan date.

They were here now. And Nathan had to bite the bullet and bring up their argument, because it wasn't fair to make Dee do it.

He was a coward, maybe, waiting until they were in a stranger's apartment surrounded by people they'd just met, but a formal sit-down hadn't felt *right*, and, if he knew Dee—which he did—he knew she'd prefer to have something to do with her hands during a difficult conversation. And this one was bound to be difficult, at least a little.

Nathan wrapped another glass and cleared his throat. "I want to apologize. What I said to you that night—it was out of line. I put my inquisitiveness over your feelings and your relationship. It wasn't fair, and I'm sorry."

Dee handed him the next glass. "Thank you. I accept your apology." She reached out and shoved his shoulder. "You were a real asshole though, and Jamie had to listen to me cry that whole weekend."

Nathan winced, not from her shove but from guilt. "I'm sorry."

"I know you are. I'm not mad. Not anymore."

"Thank you," Nathan said humbly.

Dee sighed. "I know that you weren't trying to hurt me. You were reacting to what you'd experienced—and I know it couldn't have been easy that none of us believed you."

"Hah." Nathan shook his head. "I was wrong. There wasn't anything magical happening. You met an angry cat, and I met a territorial crow. And, I guess wildfires happen."

"Yeah. But there was also the…" She pitched her voice to a low, respectful whisper. "…*body* that you found. And, well, werewolves."

True, there were werewolves.

"Do you know what the Moon illusion is?"

"Don't tell me the moon isn't real. Because if the moon isn't real, I'm out. I'm done. That's it." Nathan was only half-joking.

Dee gave him an exasperated look. "It's what they call it—"

"Who's *they*?"

"Wikipedia. Which is a reliable reference source, as *you well know*. Anyway—it's what they call it when the moon looks bigger when it's closer to the horizon and smaller when it's high in the sky." Dee helped him tape up the box and scrawled a *kitchen* label on the top and sides. "Remember that road trip we took last summer? We were driving through the mountains and the moon looked *huge*."

Nathan did remember. The moon had indeed appeared nearly ten times its usual size as they'd climbed over the mountains in his car.

"Yeah. That was awesome."

"Right? And the point is—it looked bigger. It looked like the moon was a lot closer than it ever looked when it was high up. And, if you didn't know that it wasn't, if all you were going by was what you could see, what your senses were perceiving—you'd think it was closer. No one could say that it didn't look it." She met his gaze. "You saw something that you thought was true, that seemed *unquestionably* true to you, and we didn't see it. That doesn't mean it was real," she said softly, "But it doesn't mean you should have known better, because, how could you? If I'd been in your shoes, I'd have been angry and upset as well, and probably not a little distrustful."

Nathan looked away. He wasn't proud of the rifts he'd caused in his relationships. "I'm sorry I didn't listen to you."

"It's okay. I forgive you. It wasn't your fault, Nathan. What we've gone through lately?" Dee gave an incredulous shrug. "Like, what the fuck, dude, you know?"

Nathan laughed. "Succinct," he told her.

"Thank you. I try." Dee hugged him, and Nathan nuzzled into her hair.

"By the way I gave Jamie's dad your number. He's gonna call."

"What?" Nathan jerked back. "Why? That's weird!"

"It's not weird," Dee rebuked. "He's human, just like us. And he's been through the whole, Big Reveal nonsense. He knows how trippy this is."

Nathan looked pained. "I don't want to chat with your father-in-law."

"Lowell is hilarious, so you're wrong. Besides, it'll be good for you. And he's Cole's uncle, so that makes him practically your uncle."

"In-law," Nathan corrected, weakly.

"Look." Dee cupped his face in her hands. "I'm not saying you have to bare your soul or talk about your sex life or make it weird. It just might be good to have someone who's been through this and knows what a mindfuck discovering werewolves is." She made a self-conscious face. "I've actually been Skyping with him. It started by accident—he called, and Jamie wasn't home, so we talked. And it was nice. And, I mean, he just retired from his teaching job, so he's bored, which means really you're helping out an older member of society, who—"

"Okay, okay!" Nathan held his hands up in surrender. "I'll talk to him! God." He found them another box, and Dee handed him a plate. "But only so I can hear embarrassing stories about Kiara as a baby."

"Ooh, I hadn't thought of that."

Chapter Fifty |

"I DUNNO," NATHAN SAID, FLEXING against the restraint that held his wrist to the bed. "It's never really been my thing."

"You can't say that if you've never tried it," Cole pointed out. He checked the cuff at Nathan's ankle and finding it fastened to his satisfaction, ran his hand up Nathan's bare calf. Nathan jumped at the unexpected contact, only to be stopped short by the bonds at his wrists and ankles. It sent an odd jolt through him—excitement, on the heels of a small thrill of fear. He was truly at Cole's mercy.

A frown creased Cole's forehead. "Are you sure this is okay? If it's too soon after Travis—"

"No, no." Nathan shook Cole's concern off with a wave of his hand. Or he tried to. His wrist flopped against the mattress. "This is a lot different than Travis."

And it was. Nathan knew that if he said *stop*, or *pause*, or *no*, or *hang on a sec*, at any moment that Cole would listen. Travis had been about fear and power.

Nathan supposed this was, too, but in a very different way. Cole seemed to think that Nathan could stand to give up some control, and Nathan thought that if it meant getting Cole into his bed he'd try all sorts of things. This seemed to be working, because, though Nathan lay soft against his stomach, Cole had begun to get hard the second he'd fastened a cuff around Nathan's wrist.

So here they were. Nathan's stomach jumped in anticipation when Cole crawled onto the bed with him. The mattress dipped under his weight, and Nathan's instinct was to reach for him. He was brought up short, again, by the restraints, and made a soft noise of frustration.

Cole smirked and dipped his head to slide his lips against Nathan's. The kiss was hot, wet, and messy, and when Cole finally pulled back Nathan's pupils had blown wide with desire.

"Okay." Nathan licked his lips. "There might be something to this whole tied-up business." There'd been an erotic charge, having Cole plunder his mouth while there was nothing for Nathan to do, whether to stop it or encourage it with the press of his eager hands against Cole's skin. He just had to lie there and take it.

Nathan blew out a breath when Cole rose and straddled him; Cole's weight settled heavily. Nathan wriggled under him, not from discomfort, but testing the sensations. The bonds tugged, but not unpleasantly, and Cole's thighs on either side of Nathan's torso restricted him further. Cole held a hand to each side of Nathan's face, holding him still even there, and brought his head down for another kiss.

By the time Cole pulled back, Nathan was hard and panting; his hips were rolling up to try to find some friction. Cole laughed, low and self-satisfied.

"What do you think?" He asked, reaching back with one hand to stroke Nathan's cock.

Nathan swore and arched as much as he could into the contact. "It's got potential," he said. He couldn't help but twist his arms and legs in the restraints. He wanted to move. He wanted to touch Cole. He wanted to do more than just lie there and let something happen.

"Hey, shhh." Cole ran his fingers through Nathan's hair and tugged. The sensation drew the breath from Nathan's throat. Cole's other hand continued to move on Nathan's cock. "Relax," Cole told him. "I've got you."

Nathan closed his eyes and focused on the sensations: Cole's hand wrapped firmly around him, the other tangled tight in his hair; the press of Cole's hairy, muscular thighs on either side of him; the scent, sharp and spiked with desire that even his human nose could identify. Cole sucked the lobe of Nathan's ear into his mouth. Nathan groaned; the pull was a thing he felt low in his belly.

"Atta boy," Cole said approvingly. His breath was warm and damp in Nathan's ear. Cole moved lower and brushed his lips over the delicate skin of Nathan's throat.

Nathan tensed at the initial touch. He'd worn a ring of bruises—fingerprints readily identifiable—for nearly two weeks. They'd faded, but he could still see their shadow in the mirror each morning when he shaved. Cole's tongue laved over the healing flesh, making a hot, wet line that cooled tantalizingly when Cole moved to the other side of Nathan's neck.

By the time Cole's patient mouth made it to Nathan's nipples, Nathan was writhing unselfconsciously. Something about not being able to touch Cole back heightened the sensations Cole was drawing from his body, until Nathan thought he might explode with need.

Cole bit down over Nathan's nipple and sucked it into his mouth. Nathan's eyes rolled back into his head, and he babbled pleas.

"Fuck, please, fuck me."

"You want me to fuck you?"

"Yes! God. Cole. Please." Nathan begged. He felt so unusually exposed, so helpless to Cole's whims.

Cole pinched and tugged Nathan's nipples, while Nathan's cock languished, achingly hard and untouched. Nathan whimpered in frustration; every inch of his skin seemed electrified.

"All right." Cole locked eyes with Nathan. "I'll fuck you."

Nathan shifted his hips against the mattress, trying to spread his legs wider to give Cole better access to his ass. Cole smirked and rose above Nathan before he sheathed himself onto Nathan's cock in one sudden movement.

The instant, blinding pleasure of Cole's ass clenched around his cock had Nathan staring sightless at the ceiling. His mouth gaped open; his entire body rigid as sparks flew through his veins. *Holy shit.*

Cole rocked his hips. He started slow, at first, a gentle rock that still pulled a moan from Nathan's lips. He increased the pace with each thrust, faster and faster until Nathan was certain Cole was using some of his werewolf speed.

Initially Nathan's hands ached to grip Cole's hips, to urge him on, to dig his fingers into the firm flesh. Now his entire world had narrowed until only his cock and Cole's ass existed, and every time Cole dropped down onto him Nathan cried out.

His orgasm hit like a sledgehammer. One moment Nathan was hurtling headfirst toward the ledge and the next he'd plunged over. Pleasure bowed his spine, arched his back off the bed, and drove him even deeper into Cole.

Above him, Cole grunted and took himself in hand. It only took one, two jerks and then he was coming across Nathan's face.

Nathan sank back into the mattress as the final pulses of his orgasm faded away. Cole continued to jerk himself off, and Nathan opened his mouth to catch the final few spurts. Cole tasted bitter and familiar against his tongue, and Nathan smiled dazedly when Cole finished and bent to brush a thumb through the come on Nathan's chin.

"Thank you," Cole said. He dropped a kiss onto Nathan's lips, soft and gentle, before he eased himself up and off Nathan.

He returned with a warm, wet cloth. Nathan let his eyes fall half closed as Cole cleaned him, running the cloth not just over his face, but his whole body, until Nathan's skin tingled. When he'd finished, Cole tossed the cloth into the hamper and unfastened Nathan from the bed.

"How was that?" he asked as Nathan snuggled into Cole's side.

"Good," Nathan said, surprised by how thoroughly he'd enjoyed it. Even now his body felt heavy with a pleasant lassitude, unlike anything he'd experienced.

"I can't believe you've never let anyone tie you up."

Nathan's voice was thick with sleep when he spoke. "I can't believe I'm gonna ask you to do it again."

He fell asleep with Cole's pleased chuckle rumbling against his ear.

THE MORNING SUN SPUN LAZILY through the blinds, and Nathan grumbled.

"Do you know what Kiara did when she heard about your fight with Dee?"

"Hmm?" Nathan blinked his eyes open. How did Cole know he'd woken up? Ugh. *Werewolves.*

Cole grinned. "Let me show you."

He was up and out of the bed and back again, before Nathan really had a chance to process his absence. Cole settled in with Nathan and handed over the small sculpture of the four running wolves that signified a pack registered officially with GNAAW.

Perplexed, Nathan looked from the sculpted wolves to Cole.

"Here." Cole flipped the statue over to display the base.

04/06/2017

Kiara Devon Lyons

Cole Stephen Lyons

Jamie Martineau

Taryn Nicole Lee

And, added in rough, uneven lettering:

Deanna Jacqueline Scott

Cole cleared his throat. "There's room for more. More names. Yours, if you want."

Nathan shifted his weight. "Still? I mean." He licked his lips. "Kiara'd still want me after…" *I went through a bunch of her stuff, and arranged a meeting with her arch-enemy, and lied about all of it.* He didn't think he could bring himself to say it. He'd come clean to everyone about what had happened, what he'd done. It hadn't gone so well, with Kiara storming out, Dee too disappointed to meet his eyes, and even Jamie looking more than a little pissed at Nathan's audacity. It had been the first time, too, that Cole had learned about Nathan's coffee with the Huntress.

There'd been yelling. All in all, not the best house party Nathan had thrown.

Kiara hadn't come back that night. Ryn's advice had been to let her cool off, and, true to Ryn's word, Kiara had shown up two days later to curtly inform Nathan that he was forgiven, but that if he ever did something like that again she would peel the skin off his eyeballs and make him watch while she crushed his PlayStation to dust with her bare hands.

Nathan had swallowed mutely, and that had been the last they'd spoken of it.

"Still." Cole's voice jerked Nathan out of his guilty reverie. "She loves you, you know. When people we love fuck up, that doesn't mean we stop loving them. Or wanting them."

"Right." Nathan nodded, his throat suddenly tight. He took Cole's free hand and interlocked their fingers. He stroked his other hand over the head of the lead wolf on the small statue. "I'll deserve this," he swore, meeting Cole's eyes.

"Nathan," Cole's voice was gentle with amusement, with love. "You already do."

"Yeah." Nathan swallowed past the sizable lump in his throat. "But," he sniffed "I want it professionally engraved—none of this nonsense." He waved at Kiara's scrawl, at Dee's name obviously added with the tip of a wolfish finger.

Cole stared at him. "What? Really?"

"Yeah." Nathan grinned. "And I want it in Helvetica."

"Aaand packship revoked."

"You can't do that."

"Yes, I can."

"No, you can't."

"Yes, I can."

"Don't, though."

"Hel*ve*tica?"

"Fine. Something classy like Wingdings, then."

Cole tackled Nathan to the mattress.

THE END.

Acknowledgments

I'D LIKE TO THANK TREVER and Pene and Leita, who love this pack like I do.

This one couldn't have been written without the support of my group chats:

Galentines

Vulva Pie

three girl emojis

FAM JAM

if he dies, he dies ¯_("))_/¯

BATTLE PLANS

Writing Pals

Thanks, team.

About the Author |

MICHELLE OSGOOD WRITES QUEER, FEMINIST romance from her tiny apartment in Vancouver, BC. She loves stories in all mediums, especially those created by Shonda Rhimes, and dreams of one day owning a wine cellar to rival Olivia Pope's. She is active in Vancouver's poly and LGBTQ communities, never turns down a debate about pop culture, and is trying to learn how to cook. Her novels *The Better to Kiss You With* (2016) and *Huntsmen* (2017) were published by Interlude Press.

Also by **Michelle Osgood**

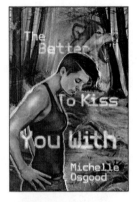

The Better to Kiss You With
The Better to Kiss You With series, Book One

Deanna, the moderator for Wolf's Run, an online werewolf role-playing game, wanders the local forest with her dog Arthur and daydreams about Jamie, the attractive, enigmatic woman who lives upstairs. When threats from an antagonistic player escalate, Deanna wonders if her job could be riskier than she'd ever imagined—and if her new girlfriend knows more about this community than she had realized.

ISBN (print) 978-1-941530-74-0 | (eBook) 978-1-941530-75-7

Huntsmen
The Better to Kiss You With series, Book Two

Kiara is stunned to run into her ex, Taryn. But before she can react, she's warned they're in danger. The Huntsmen, a group of werewolf-tracking humans, is scouring the city for lone werewolves like Taryn. As they wait for help from Kiara's pack, the women face the differences that drove them apart and fear the Huntsmen may not be acting alone.

ISBN (print) 978-1-945053-19-1 | (eBook) 978-1-945053-33-7

You may **also** like...

Curved Horizon by Tayor Brooke
The Camellia Clock Cycle, Book Two

Picking up a few weeks after the conclusion of Fortitude Smashed. Daisy and Chelsea Cavanaugh try find a way to transform their friendship into something more, while Shannon and Aiden celebrate their one-year anniversary and deal with a horrific accident that puts Shannon's life at risk.

ISBN (print) 978-1-945053-54-2 | (eBook) 978-1-945053-55-9

One **story**
can change **everything.**

@interlude**press**

Twitter | Facebook | Instagram | Pinterest | Tumblr

For a reader's guide to **Moon Illusion** *and book club prompts,
please visit interludepress.com.*

CPSIA information can be obtained
at www.ICGtesting.com
Printed in the USA
FFOW03n1200170418
46237053-47613FF

9 781945 053566